Tunnel Vision

Tunnel Vision

by Peter Lerangis

AN
APPLE
PAPERBACK

SCHOLASTIC INC.
New York Toronto London Auckland Sydney
Mexico City New Delhi Hong Kong Buenos Aires

ISBN 0-439-50728-6

Text copyright © 2005 by Peter Lerangis.

All rights reserved. Published by Scholastic Inc.
SCHOLASTIC, APPLE PAPERBACKS, and associated logos are trademarks
and/or registered trademarks of Scholastic Inc.

Design by Tim Hall

12 11 10 9 8 7 6 5 4 3 2   5 6 7 8 9 10/0
Printed in the U.S.A.   40
First printing, May 2005

This book and all the
Spy X *books are dedicated to Kendra*
Levin, whose wonderful idea set
Andrew and Evie in motion.

Tunnel Vision

Chapter One

It was happening fast. Too fast.

He wanted it to stop. He wanted a magic hand to freeze time, to give him a chance to think. Because none of it made sense.

His mind was screaming: *I am in an underground tunnel. My sister and I have found Mom, who has been missing for ten months. The three of us are tucked into a crevice, hiding from an enemy who is in the same room. The enemy is with our father.*

Andrew Wall's mind could play tricks. He knew that. Everyone knew it. To Andrew, there was no *normal* in everyday life. A bike ride was a dangerous flight mission, the walk to homeroom a galactic battle. His twin sister, Evie, said his imagination was like his hair. It always needed trimming.

But this was real life. And it was way weirder than anything Andrew had ever made up in his nearly twelve years on earth.

A familiar deep voice echoed in the cold darkness: "Do you see anything in there?"

Andrew could feel Evie trembling. He wanted the voice to be someone else's, just like she did. He wanted to think, *Phew, it only sounded like Pop.* But as Andrew watched a flashlight beam swing wildly through the cavern, he could see the athletic, ramrod-straight shape of the man that matched the voice.

It was Pop. No question.

Here they were, the entire Wall family. Together for the first time in nearly a year — since the morning Mom left home, back when they lived in another state. It was a day Andrew and Evie called "11 11 11": the eleventh day of the eleventh month, on their eleventh birthday. Mom's present to them that morning was a good-bye note. In it was a secret code. That code started them on the path to finding her. Tonight, after weeks of secret spy training, car chases, a cross-country move, a showdown in a cable-car museum, a kidnap attempt in a tunnel under Alcatraz, and a brush with enemy spies near the Golden Gate Bridge, the path had ended.

But it wasn't exactly the family reunion Andrew had been dreaming about. Part of him — the little-kid part — wanted to jump up and down. To leap out of the shadows at Pop and say, "Boo!" Then Mom and Pop would hug and kiss, and they'd all climb back to street level and have a late-night breakfast at IHOP.

But he knew that was impossible. Pop was not alone.

Another voice called out, this one from inside a passageway to their left: "Nothing yet. This place goes on forever. Be careful. It's wet."

That was Marisol. The college student Pop had hired as their nanny.

Only she wasn't a nanny. Or a college student. She was a spy who worked for a corrupt government intelligence agency called The Company, which was chasing Mom. Andrew and Evie had trusted Marisol. They'd showed her a coded message from Mom. The messages had been coming for weeks, most of them tucked into boxes full of spy equipment. It had all been part of Mom's master plan: to train Andrew and Evie to become spies and rescue her.

It might have worked, too. But now the plan was toast. Andrew and Evie had blown it. Mom had instructed them to keep the messages secret, to trust no one. Because they had blabbed to Marisol, their secret was out. Instead of spies, they were targets. They'd nearly been kidnapped by The Company.

If it weren't for The Resistance, they might all be dead. The Resistance had rescued Mom and smuggled her into their headquarters in the tunnels below the Presidio, a former military base that was now a national park. Mom had been forced to summon Andrew and Evie, to keep them from harm.

That was how the twins had found her. They'd found her in spite of themselves. Without a plan. Without safe-guards.

And so they'd been followed. By Marisol. Which meant The Company knew where they were. And The Company would show no mercy, to Mom or her kids.

Or to Pop.

"Hang on a second," Pop called out to Marisol. "I'm not as young or as fast as you!"

Why was he here? With her? Andrew's mind raced, trying to figure out how Pop could have ended up here: Back home, he would have noticed Andrew and Evie were gone. He would have gone to Andrew's bedroom and looked around. There he'd see the image of the Golden Gate Bridge that Andrew had left on his computer screen — the image The Company had sent Andrew to lure him into a trap. Pop would have gone to the bridge, hoping to find Andrew. That must have been where he met Marisol. Pop still thought Marisol was a harmless college kid. She could easily have talked him into coming down here — *I know where your kids are, follow me!*

And now Andrew and Evie had not only put Mom's life in danger, but Pop's, too. Not to mention the entire Resistance.

They'd have to do something about Marisol — drive her out, capture her, *something*.

Most of all, Pop and Mom needed to talk. He believed that she couldn't be trusted. That The Company was a legitimate government organization, which Mom had betrayed. Mom told a different story. Yes, she had worked for The Company, and yes, it was once the secret, elite intelligence wing of the U. S. government, the "code breakers' code breakers." But that was before she discovered The Company's secret murders, the plans for government takeover. After that, she was marked for death and had to flee.

Who was right? Should Andrew believe Pop? Pop was smart. He worked for the government in covert operations. He had contact with The Company — sometimes he even reported to their headquarters on business. But they were smart, too. They would have fed him plenty of spin. Turned his mind against Mom.

In the messages Mom had sent Andrew and Evie, she had included instructions not to tell Pop anything. Which made sense. The Company would have an eye on him. Keeping him in the dark would protect him.

Now Pop was in the thick of it. Did The Company plan to kidnap him, too?

They had to lie low. Marisol might have a gun. Andrew silently hoped that Mom had some secret strategy to isolate Pop.

Pop made one last sweep of the underground room with his flashlight, revealing the smooth circular cement tunnel, the roots growing through cracks overhead, the green-blue water stain down the opposite wall.

It was cold down here. Cold and wet and creepy. Andrew tried to shrink further into the crevice, but the beam passed safely overhead. Pop moved toward the passageway, to the part of the tunnel complex that Marisol was exploring. He disappeared through a narrow archway.

The light flickered dimly. In a moment the room was dark again.

"We have to get him!" Andrew whispered, his voice echoing like the rustle of dry leaves.

He felt Mom's hand on his mouth, shushing him. He shivered. When was the last time she had done *that*? In a fraction of a second, Andrew felt a rush of memories — of smiled *Good morning*s and slumped-shouldered *Do your homework*s, of a thousand different *Mom* moves that said a thousand things. He knew now, somehow, that they weren't really different at all but a thousand ways of saying I love you, and despite the danger, he threw his arms around her and held tight. Because nothing mattered more than this, that she was back — and being with her in a cold dark tunnel was better than being anywhere else without her.

Mom hugged him hard, and Andrew could feel Evie's arms, too. All three of them, silent and rocking, gently rocking. He wished he could *see* them. But in a moment Mom was guiding Andrew's left hand, placing his index finger through a belt loop in Evie's jeans. When Evie lurched forward, pulled by Mom, Andrew followed.

His feet nearly gave out beneath him.

"Walk much?" his sister whispered.

Andrew smiled. Evie could be obnoxious. She had been born four minutes before him. That meant, in her mind, that she was the "smarter, older" sister. But he could forgive her for that. Right now, he could forgive her for anything.

The three of them were a chain now, with Mom in front. They moved quickly in the direction Pop had gone. Mom had a flashlight, but she didn't dare turn it on. She seemed to know the tunnel well. It was pitch-dark, and instinctively Andrew reached out with his right hand.

He smacked a hard dirt wall, then he felt upward to the ceiling, which was only a few inches over his head. He tried to stay on tiptoe, but that was hard to do leaning forward, and his feet splashed through the meandering trickle of water that seemed to be everywhere.

As they rounded a sharp corner, a beam of light appeared. Mom stopped short. The light passed quickly across them.

Then it snapped back to their faces.

"There they are!"

Marisol.

Evie jerked away, and Andrew's finger came loose. But Mom had him by the arm now, and she was pushing him and his sister in the opposite direction.

He stumbled back around the corner, back into darkness. Back to the place where the light couldn't reach. Evie let out a scream. He heard her land on the floor.

"My ankle!" she groaned.

Andrew knelt. Mom was shoulder-to-shoulder with him now, both of them reaching down, pulling Evie up.

Andrew could hear Pop and Marisol coming closer. In moments they would be making the turn. He hooked his sister's arm around his shoulder.

"Andrew?" Pop's voice called from around the corner. "Evie?"

Andrew swallowed back an answer. His instinct was to answer. He always answered Pop.

But everything now was a fight against instinct. Instinct and logic.

He heard a whooshing sound directly ahead. He felt a rush of cold air. Mom was yanking him, and he held tight to his sister.

They moved sharply to the right — where there ought to have been a wall. But there was only empty space. They passed through and the whooshing repeated itself, behind them now.

They stood still, panting for breath. The tunnel's shape slowly appeared around them, with a strange glow. It was less like light than a softening of darkness.

"Andrewwwww . . . !"

The sound of Pop's voice, muffled and distant, made Andrew flinch. Still holding onto his sister, Andrew turned to look over his shoulder. Behind them was a solid rock wall. "We passed through that?" he murmured.

Evie winced with pain. "It's a *door*. A sliding door."

"The rock is cragged," Mom said, her eyes trained on the wall. "To the naked eye, in poor lighting, it's nearly impossible to see the door's outline. We're safe for now, but we have to get to the Command Center. Are you okay, Evie?"

"Sort of," Evie said. "I mean, no. Yes. I mean . . ." She looked up at Mom, struggling for words, her eyes moist. "I missed you — *so much*."

Mom swept her up in a hug, and Andrew leaned his head against them. He had a million things to tell her — about good grades and bad, new friends made, travel stories, adventures. Ten months of bottled-up thoughts and questions. He'd vowed to unload it all, the moment they finally met. But now that the moment was here, now that he could finally talk, all he could think to say was, "When are we going to get Pop back? When can we all be together?"

"First let's get Evie to a doctor," Mom said. "We have several of them here. Good ones. Can you walk, sweetie?"

"I think my ankle is broken," Evie replied, "and my knee hurts."

"Is either of them swollen?" Mom asked.

Evie lifted her pant leg. She moved her leg to the left and right. Her birthmark, a dull little mark on the back of her right leg, winked at her. Andrew had a similar mark on his left leg, which he tried to wash off with Comet once when he was a kid. He laughed aloud at the memory of Mom's flabbergasted reaction, which hadn't seemed funny at the time. "What's so hilarious?" Evie snapped.

"Nothing!" Andrew sputtered. "I don't know. I'm in a good mood. I was just —"

"At least the knee's okay," Evie said, rolling down her pants. "For now."

Mom gave her a sympathetic look and put Evie's free arm around her shoulder. They began moving forward. Supported by both Mom and Andrew, Evie hopped gingerly on her good foot. "I don't like this place," Evie said.

"Neither do I," Mom replied with a sigh. "But we're building other facilities, in other cities. Nicer ones, I hope. We have to keep up with The Company, and they are a sprawling beast. Their whole organization is built on surprise. Being one step ahead. That was always their mission, even back in the seventeen hundreds when they began."

"Whoa," Andrew said. "They're *four hundred* years old?"

"Three hundred," Evie corrected him.

"Even then," Mom said, "they knew that in order to survive, you had to seek out the craftiest enemies of the Republic, the most original evil minds — and hire them. Pay them to figure out ways to subvert the government. The Company was like a laboratory — they'd out-think the real enemies, to stop them before they even started."

"Like businesses who hire hackers to crack their own codes," Evie said.

"Exactly," Mom replied. "And the system worked, more or less, for years. But the problem is, when you hire bad eggs, it's not good for the omelette. When The Company started killing off its enemies during the Cold War, they kept it secret. They lied. The victims had been 'relocated.' When I found out what they were doing, I couldn't work for them anymore. Not if I valued my life. Or the ideals of my country."

Mom let her words hang in the air. Suddenly, she stopped. Andrew stopped with her, his shoulder aching from Evie's weight. Her eyes filled with tears. "Has it really been ten months?" she asked.

"It feels like ten years," Evie said, burying her face in Mom's shoulder. "But we'll be a family again, right? We'll find Pop?"

"Yes, we'll be a family," Mom replied softly.

She led them to a steel door at the end of the corridor, then inserted a passcard. The door slowly swung open, into an enormous vaulted room. But Andrew noticed only one thing.

Pop's eyes. Staring directly into his.

Chapter Two

Andrew gasped.

Pop's face loomed down from a giant monitor that seemed to float overhead, hanging from the roof of the domed chamber. What was his image doing there? *Where were they?*

Andrew slowly took in the surroundings. He, Evie, and Mom were standing on a raised circular platform, above what seemed like a city of people crowded into one room. They sat in messy cubicles, huddled over cramped control panels or poised over keyboards. The floor was littered with soda cans and candy wrappers.

Andrew scanned the personnel — a surfer dude with a tank top and deep tan, a rail-thin elderly man with no hair, a green-haired middle-aged woman, a slacker girl with a bowl cut and a plaid retro skirt. Punkers sat next to hackers, uptown types next to grunge babies. Leaning against the wall, looking as if he'd wandered in from school, was a kid about Andrew's age. And in the middle of the floor, wearing a backward baseball cap, was a small, wiry woman with a runner's physique and close-cropped dark hair. She was shouting into a cell phone. The whole scene was a slice of San Francisco, sunk underground. All of them were looking up at Pop's face on the monitor.

"They're isolating him," Mom said, "and the agent. Marisol."

"Who's they?" Evie asked.

"Welcome, Andrew and Evie, to The Resistance," Mom said with a weary smile.

Andrew gazed over the room. "This is *it*?"

"CCM2," Mom replied. "Control Center, Minotaur II. Fondly known as The Pit. This room is the guts of our operation. You were expecting it to look different?"

Andrew shrugged. He *had* expected something else. Men and women dressed in black, maybe. Sleek steel walls and polished floors. Tom Cruise racing urgently across the floor, loaded with gadgets.

He expected The Resistance to be heroes, fighting evil and corruption. Like the Revolutionary War minutemen, only with women, too. The smartest of the smart. At least that's how Mom had described them. Hey, they had set up a totally secret set of tunnels in the midst of a huge city, right under the enemy's nose. It was called Minotaur II, according to Foxglove, Mom's code-breaking teacher who'd guided them to the tunnel entrance. Originally it was meant to be an extension of The Company's tunnel system, an ancient one that ran from the Bay to Chinatown. But when The Company's entire construction team went over to The Resistance, they took the secret of Minotaur II's location with them — and developed it without anyone finding out.

What kind of people did stuff like that? Geniuses. Good guys. Heroes.

"But they're, like, so normal," Andrew said.

Mom had set Evie down gently in a chair and was examining her ankle. "Well, you'll have to pardon their rudeness, Andrew," she said. "They're busy watching Pop."

Overhead, Pop's face loomed closer, distorted by the lens. His nose fattened and then shrank to normal as he looked away. "*Where did they go*?" he shouted over his shoulder, his voice booming through the speakers.

Offscreen, Marisol's voice replied, "Let's try this way!" Pop's face retreated, and the screen went dark.

A murmur of relief swept through the room.

"What luck," Mom said, glancing at the monitor over her shoulder. "I don't think he saw it."

"Saw what?" Evie asked.

"The lens," Mom replied. "He was staring right into one. There are hundreds of them embedded in the walls. Tiny. Like little pieces of quartz. Agent Optikon — the skinny guy with the comb-over, who's eating elbow noodles — he's an ocular expert, an optician in his former life. He went a little wild on the design. But as a result, we have every inch of the complex covered." She pointed to the left. "That's what you see over there."

Andrew turned toward the left wall, where dozens of smaller monitors glowed floor-to-ceiling with darkened images of the tunnel complex.

Two figures — Pop and Marisol — dashed diagonally across one of the monitors and disappeared, only to reappear on the next monitor moments later.

"Center Quadrant Four!" Agent Optikon called out, his mouth full of noodles.

The woman with the cell phone shouted in reply: "SEAL TUNNEL SEVENTEEN, OPEN FILLMORE SHUNT, DIVERT AND ISOLATE TO SOUTHWEST QUADRANT, PACIFIC EGRESS!"

Fingers clicked furiously on keyboards. The monitor images flickered. In one, Andrew could see a door sliding shut. In another, a door opened.

"I NEED AN ONYX VIEW, STAT!" the woman barked.

The big overhead screen, which had gone dark, came back to life. Now it showed an electronic map of complex pathways — the whole Minotaur II tunnel system. A set of glowing electronic dots moved through the paths.

"It's like Pac-Man," Andrew murmured.

"It's a schematic map of the Minotaur II tunnels in present time, using a global-positioning technology based on the infrared spectrum," Mom said. "The Onyx system, we call it. And those two dots are Richard and Marisol."

"We're watching them go through the tunnel?" Evie asked.

"We're controlling where they go," Mom replied. "By manipulating the pathway choices."

The two dots traveled up a white corridor, which suddenly went bright red behind them. To their left, another pathway went red. "Red means we've sealed off the pathway," Mom continued. "Sliding rock doors, like the ones you saw. We can open and seal sections of the tunnel complex at will. They will be forced to exit onto Pacific Avenue."

"You're letting Marisol escape?" Andrew asked. "With Pop? What if The Company kidnaps him? And what if they come back here? They'll know exactly where Minotaur II is —"

"This makes me sick," Evie murmured as she watched the screen. "They're treating Pop like . . . like a rat! Why are you letting them do this, Mom?"

"Marisol is the rat," Andrew blurted out. "She's probably going to try to brainwash him. Or maybe even, like, reprogram his DNA. To take him over to the Dark Side. He already thinks Mom isn't to be —"

Trusted.

Andrew didn't dare finish the sentence in front of Mom. He glanced at her sheepishly, but her eyes were fixed on the overhead monitor, watching the progress of the dots. Nearly all the paths were red now. Pop and Marisol had progressed to the bottom of the screen.

"They're out," she said under her breath. "They're out!"

A roar welled up, loud and sudden. Agent Optikon let out a whoop, punching his fist in the air and spilling his noodles. Surfer dude jumped up and danced, and slacker girl high-fived the old guy.

Mom turned to Evie. "Time to get you some professional care." She tapped loudly on a metal banister that encircled the room. "*Hello, everyone! I have good news. I found my kids — and we could sure use Dr. Merwin!*"

The many faces turned her way, finally distracted from the overhead monitor — and the ruckus suddenly swelled again. People came out from inside their cubicles. They surrounded Mom, congratulating her. A hundred hands reached out to shake Andrew's and Evie's. The older guy started singing "For they are jolly good fellows" at the top of his lungs, and a couple of other voices joined in.

"Hi," Andrew said again and again. The people were happy, triumphant even — but he didn't feel that way at all. He felt as if he were in a long, horrible dream. Plus the room was sticky and cold. "Hi . . . hi . . . yes, I'm Andrew . . . Andrew Wall . . . thanks . . . yeah, I know I look like her . . ."

As he shook hands, he noticed a pair of eyes sizing him up from a distance, from the edge of the crowd. It was the boy, the one who'd been hanging out by the wall. How strange to see someone his age here.

"Yeeeowwww!"

Andrew felt the bones of his right hand scrunch together as if they'd been squashed in a vise.

The woman with the baseball cap pumped his hand. "Glad you made it, Andrew, pleased to meet you," she said. Her dark eyes were as powerful as her grip.

"Thanks," Andrew replied as she finally let go. "I think."

Mom walked up behind her. "This is the boss," she said. "We call her Two. As in Number Two."

"Who's Number One?" Andrew asked.

"*We could tell you that — but then we'd have to shoot you,*" said a chorus of Resistance workers in unison.

Andrew pretended to smile. He hated that joke. Mom and Pop used to make it all the time.

Two glared at the workers. "OKAY, BACK TO WORK!" she snapped. "We have a Class One breach. I want damage assessments. Hard copies of all intercepts, all Company chatter — and there *will* be chatter. Methuselah, I want you to begin Disable Procedure, Tunnel 24S Pacific, stat. Prepare preliminary Code White, effacement operation —"

"Effacement?" the older man said.

"I SAID *PRELIMINARY.* NOW MOVE." As the man doddered away, along with the others, Two shrugged. "Sometimes you have to treat them like children. Now, come. I need to ask you and your sister some questions."

Doctor Merwin, who'd wrapped Evie's ankle in an Ace bandage, smiled confidently. "Only a sprain," he said.

"Good," Two replied, squatting next to Evie. "Now, tell me. How *exactly* did you two get here?"

Andrew and Evie nearly tripped over each other telling her the story. Their narrow escape from The Company in a tunnel under Alcatraz. The cell phone message that lured Andrew to the Golden Gate Bridge, where Marisol was waiting with another Company spy. Evie's realization that some of the boxes they'd been receiving were not from Mom but from The Company, and that Andrew had been tricked. Her attempt to rescue him. The chase through the Presidio, where they were found by their Resistance pals, Foxglove and Mr. and Mrs. Franklin. The escape into Minotaur II, with Pop close behind.

Two listened carefully and nodded. "Okay, so it seems they saw just the one entrance. That's good. That buys a little time. We can close that entrance permanently — and the one where they escaped. That's the beauty of Minotaur II. We can afford to sacrifice certain branches of the tunnel system — fill them in and make it seem that they never existed. But it'll be a temporary measure at best. I want you to think hard — is there anything else we need to worry about? Any clues you may have left behind? Anything The Company might get a hold of? Because it's certain they'll be heading to your house right now."

Of course, Andrew thought. *Marisol will want to know everything. And Pop will trust her.* He looked nervously at Evie. "You mean, like codes? And spy equipment?"

"And maps!" Evie added. "All of that stuff — it's just sitting in boxes. There's a whole map of Minotaur II — the one you sent us, Mom!"

"Where are those boxes?" Mom asked.

Andrew swallowed hard. "In my closet," he said softly.

Two rose slowly to her feet. "Detailed maps?" she asked.

"I sent them the Stage Four overlay with an unmarked street map," Mom replied.

"So if you put the two together, you get the whole system," Two murmured. "Every nook and cranny . . ."

"What'll happen if Marisol finds it?" Andrew asked.

"How do you know they'll even *go* there?" Evie said. "They might be in the Presidio, looking for another way into the tunnel."

"Are we at Code White?" Mom asked.

"Maybe," Two replied.

"What does Code White mean?" Evie said.

"Hang on to your seat belts." Two turned away, shouting into her cell phone. "GET ME MAD MIKE!"

From The Pit, someone started running to the platform.

"Look, I know exactly where those boxes are," Andrew said. "I could go back and get them right now —"

"*We* could," Evie reminded him.

But Two ignored them. She was talking to someone at the top of the stairs. — the boy Andrew had seen in the crowd. His dark hair was gelled and combed forward and his expression seemed stuck between a sneer and a smirk. *This* was Mad Mike?

"We need an interception on Jackson Street," Two was telling him.

"When?" Mike asked.

"Five minutes ago," Two replied. "Andrew and Evie will give you details. Be nice to them. Now MOVE!"

Andrew couldn't believe this. *Mike* was going to the house — to Andrew's bedroom? "But — but — but I —"

"Uh, hel-*lo*?" Mike said, rolling his eyes. "Do we speak English here?"

Chapter Three

"I hate him," Andrew said.

"Hate is bad." Evie stared at a computer screen, scratching her head. Andrew was obsessed with Mad Mike. Mom had patiently explained that Mike was a double agent. The Company thought he was one of them — so he'd be safe if he did run into Marisol or Pop. And Evie didn't seem to care that he'd be going through all their stuff.

She was busy with a computer. Mom had left them here, in a small room with white walls, a fluorescent overhead light, two chairs, a half-dozen battered file cabinets, and a desk with an old Dell computer. ISCD, it was called. Intelligence Section, Codes Division.

It was more like a closet, Evie thought.

She missed Mom already. Finding her had taken *ten months*. She expected at least a few hours of undivided Mom-ness. Especially after a mad chase through a drafty tunnel on a bum ankle. But Mom had stayed with them all of a half hour. They'd laughed and cried and reminisced, but it wasn't enough. There were so many things Evie wanted to know — like what Mom's life had been like, how she had managed to track them down and plant all those boxes, and, most important, how exactly they were going to rescue Pop. But the conversation hadn't gotten that far. Mom had "work to do." It was all-hands-on-deck, she explained, now that The Company knew about Minotaur II. With apologies and a promise that she'd be back soon, she left for The Pit. Andrew and Evie were supposed to "help" by continuing their spy training. Formally. With The Resistance's official code-training program.

Which meant Evie was stuck in a musty old room, trying to concentrate while her brother paced back and forth. Andrew Wall, Annoying at All Costs. He was staring at his cell phone, waiting for a text message from Mad Mike, who was supposed to contact them when he got to the Walls' house.

"She could have sent us to the house instead of him," Andrew blurted out. "I mean, we *live* there."

"We're not double agents," Evie asked. "And we're not twenty-one-year-old professional spies."

"Well, he looks like he's twelve," Andrew grumped.

Evie sighed. "Look, if you're worried he'll take the super-size Chunkies hidden behind the pile of shoes in your closet, don't be. I ate the last one."

"*How did you find those?*"

"I owe you," Evie said. "Now, are you finished freaking out? If you are, maybe you can help me access this site."

"How can you think of code breaking at a time like this?" Andrew asked.

"Because I have to," Evie said. "Because if I don't, I'm going to go crazy wondering when Mom is coming back. It's like, *boom*, we see her — and *boom*, she's gone! I need a distraction, okay?"

"Good point." Andrew leaned over her shoulder and looked at the screen:

Official Resistance code training program.

(Password must be digital form of user name.)

User name B. Hegad

Password

ENTER

"Your user name is B. Hegad?" he asked.

"No," Evie said. "But watch this." She highlighted the name and pressed DELETE, but the name bounced right back. "I can't get rid of it."

"Maybe you're not supposed to," Andrew said. "Maybe you're just supposed to leave it."

"Okay, so then what's the password? And why is that line running uphill?"

Andrew shrugged. "Good spies make bad Web designers, I guess."

"Some help," Evie said. "Would you please go and get Mom?"

"You are *so* inside the box, Evie," Andrew said. "Think about it. Mom leaves us here but forgets to tell us the password — which is totally unlike her."

"So?"

"So, she must be testing us. This is part of the training. We're supposed to figure out the password ourselves!"

"Hmmm. You think B. Hegad could be some kind of code — like an anagram?"

"What do you get if you scramble the letters?" Andrew began scribbling on a legal pad. "Let's see . . . H. Badge . . . had beg . . . bed hag?"

"There must be something else." Evie glanced at the

screen and read aloud: "'Password must be digital form of user name.' What does *that* mean?"

"Isn't everything digital in a computer?" Andrew asked.

"It depends what you mean by digital," Evie said. "Digital could be referring to *digits*. Numbers. Mom loves number tricks."

"Math?" Andrew's face went pale.

"Maybe easy math." Evie stared at the name. "B is one letter. Hegad is five."

Andrew typed 1 and 5 above the password line.

PASSWORD INVALID.

"I know," Andrew said. "What about each letter's place in the alphabet? You know, B is the second letter, so we replace it with two, and H with eight . . ." He wrote out the results on the paper:

$$2\ 85\ 7|4$$

"Those numbers look familiar," Evie said.

Andrew nodded. "I think they won the Lotto last week."

Evie thought back to their house in Connecticut, before

they'd moved to San Francisco. Back where it all began. Their next-door neighbor, a mysterious old lady named Mrs. Digitalis, turned out to be Agent Foxglove. She had taught Andrew and Evie the basics of code breaking.

Including number patterns.

"Remember Foxglove's coded message that didn't really mean anything — unless you read every sixth word?" Evie asked. "First you had to decode a *key*. That was the only way you could read the message. It looked something like this . . ." She grabbed a pen and jotted something on paper.

$$A = .5$$
$$B = .333$$
$$C = .25$$
$$D = .2$$
$$E = .1666$$

"Right!" Andrew said. "There would be a letter at the beginning, in some place pretty obvious. If it was A, that meant one-half — so you read every other word. B key was one-third — every third word. Next is one-fourth —"

"Then one-fifth, and one-sixth," Evie continued. "Now, do you remember the decimal form for one-seventh?"

"Wait — wait!" Andrew thought for a moment. "Uh, no."

"It's this."

$$.142857$$

"You *remember* that?" Andrew asked.

"It's a recurring pattern with any fraction that has seven in the denominator," Evie said, continuing to write carefully. "As you change the numerator, you put the first digit to the end of the line and the others move forward. So, let's say you start with this . . ."

$$.142857 = \tfrac{1}{7}$$

"If you move the one to the end," she continued, "you get another 'seventh' fraction."

$$.428571 = \tfrac{3}{7}$$

"And if you move the four to the end, still another."

$$.285714 = \tfrac{2}{7}$$

"And so on . . ."

$$.857142 = \tfrac{6}{7}$$
$$.571428 = \tfrac{4}{7}$$

A slow smile spread across Andrew's face. "Hey, the third one on our list —"

"Is the same sequence as B. Hegad," Evie replied. "Exactly."

"Two-sevenths," Andrew said. "Which means that the slanted password line under B. Hegad could be a *fraction* line!"

Evie quickly moved the cursor on the screen and typed in two numbers:

Official Resistance code training program.

(Password must be digital form of user name.)

User name __B. Hegad_____

Password $\dfrac{2}{7}$

ENTER

Evie triumphantly clicked the ENTER button.

PASSWORD INVALID.

She groaned. "That's impossible! I worked it out so carefully."

Andrew glanced over the notes and smiled. "Not carefully enough. You're missing . . . the point."

"What?"

With a flourish, Andrew wrote on the paper:

$$B.\ Hegad = 2.85714$$

"The point is . . . *the point!*" Andrew said. "The period after the initial B. Which becomes a decimal point. Which changes the fraction."

Andrew changed Evie's password from 2/7 to 20/7, and clicked ENTER. The screen image dissolved, giving way to a big, bold CONGRATULATIONS!

They watched as another image appeared:

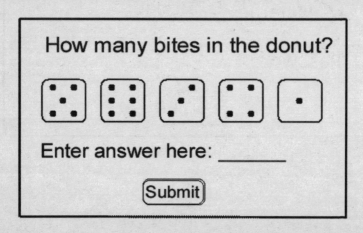

"Okay, Einstein, go for it," Evie said.

Andrew scrunched his eyes at the screen. "*Donut*? Those look like dice."

"It's some kind of game," Evie said. "Bites . . . bites?"

"Like *bytes*? As in megabytes and gigabytes?"

"Too complicated. I think it could mean the number of dots. Twenty-four . . . try that!"

Andrew entered 24 on the line and pressed Submit.

WRONG. THERE ARE <u>6</u> BITES IN THE DONUT. TRY AGAIN? YES NO

"Six?" Evie said. "How do they see six?"

"Wait. Let me write down the pattern and the answer." Andrew carefully copied the patterns and the correct number. "Let's keep guessing. We can compare the right answers. Sooner or later we'll get it."

Evie clicked YES and another screen popped up:

How many bites in the donut?

Enter answer here: _____

Submit

"Maybe the answer is a number pattern." Evie said. "Like the *differences* between each. Okay, the difference between the first pair is two. The difference between the second pair is also two. Then three. Then two. So if you add them all up . . . two, two, three, two . . ."

"Nine!" Andrew blurted out. "What a genius!"

Evie reached over and typed in 9.

WRONG. THERE ARE <u>2</u> BITES IN THE DONUT.
TRY AGAIN? YES NO

"*Two?*" Evie said.

"We stink," Andrew sighed.

"Copy it down," Evie replied.

They tried two more:

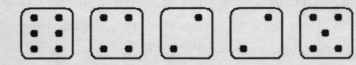

whose answer was 4, and

which was 8.

"B. Hegad was much easier," Evie said, shaking her head.

"It's impossible. Time for a break." Andrew minimized the screen. He typed furiously for a moment and a window popped up, showing a complicated structure. "Now, this is cool."

"Andrew, what are you doing?" Evie asked.

"It's an Explorer window. It's the structure of the system, Evie. Hey, check this out — they have a wireless network, like we do at home!"

"Andrew, that's none of our business!"

She lunged for the mouse. Andrew pulled it away. Laughing, he rolled back in his chair. The mouse cord went taut. It slipped from his fingers and fell onto the keyboard with a loud clatter.

Suddenly the screen blacked out.

"Oh, great, look what you've done now!" Evie said.

"It wasn't my fault," Andrew said. "You were the one who —"

Beep. Beep. Beep.

A full-screen message glared from the screen:

EMERGENCY CODE ACTIVATED.

ENTIRE SYSTEM WILL BE DELETED.

HARD DRIVE DATA UPLOADING NOW ...

Chapter Four

"*Andrew, what did you just do?*" Evie shouted.

Andrew stared at the screen dumbfounded. "Nothing."

"A system wipeout is not nothing! We were supposed to *save* Mom — not destroy everything she stands for!"

"It's not being destroyed," Andrew said. "It's going somewhere. It's uploading to another location."

"Oh, great, Andrew!" Evie asked. "You let a hacker get into the system."

She rose to her feet, wincing at the pain in her ankle, and pulled the door open.

"Will you stop it?" Andrew jumped up and stood in the entrance. "Listen, Evie. *Just listen*!"

A steady murmuring from The Pit filtered down the hallway. Evie cocked her head. "What am I supposed to hear?"

"Screaming, alarm bells — *I don't know*!" Andrew replied. "If something was wrong, we'd *hear* it!"

"They haven't found out yet!"

"They are in front of their computers, and they're really, really smart. We don't need to tell them anything.

Evie, what if they're doing it on purpose — and we're not supposed to know?" Andrew pulled the door shut. "Look, I didn't hack into the data files. I wouldn't know how. I mean, you and I are good at codes, but — reality check — we're still on Level One of the training program. All I did was view the network connection properties. Which means I was just *seeing* stuff. I saw the data being transferred. The Resistance is deleting its files and sending them somewhere else!"

"Why would they do that? Where would they be sending it?"

"Security was breached, right? So maybe they're sending the data someplace else for safekeeping."

Evie sank down into a chair, staring at the computer screen. "Maybe you're right. I don't know, Andrew. I'm really jumpy. This whole place gives me the creeps. Especially this room. I want to go home."

"So do I," Andrew grumbled, "but they sent Mad Mike instead."

"I want our old life back, Andrew," Evie said, her eyes growing misty. "Are we ever going back up? Will Mom ever come back with us? Are things ever going to be the way they were?"

"We're in a battle, Evie," Andrew replied. "We're trying to defeat The Company and keep the country safe!"

"I thought that's why we had a president and a military," Evie shot back. "The country is in big trouble if they have to count on these people. They're weird and geeky and pale and they live underground."

"Mom isn't weird and geeky."

"How do we know they haven't brainwashed her? I mean, she hasn't seen us for almost a year, and she's with *them*! How do we *know* they're not the bad guys?"

"Okay, okay. Look, my head is totally messed up by this too. We can't know anything for sure. You're right about that. But we don't have any *evidence* that The Resistance are bad guys. As for The Company . . ." Andrew began counting on his fingers. "One. They ransacked Mrs. Digitalis's house and tracked her down. Two. They sent Marisol to spy on us. Three. They sent us boxes of clues to fake us out. Four. They trapped us under Alcatraz and nearly kidnapped us. Five. They lured us to the Golden Gate Bridge, then chased us into Minotaur II. Six. They dragged Pop into this —"

"That's what it *seems* like, Andrew. But we could have been fooled. Almost every time we think we've figured something out, we're wrong. Look, Pop warned us about Mom. He said we couldn't trust her."

"But he was wrong!"

"So he lied to us? Is that what you're saying? Our own father?"

"He didn't know," Andrew said. "He was fooled."

"He's not that stupid," Evie replied.

"So you're saying Mom's lying? How can you just assume Pop's right?"

"*He isn't the one who left us.*"

Andrew had a reply all prepared, but it stuck in his mouth.

A soft beep sounded from his pants pocket. He pulled out his cell phone. A text message appeared on the screen:

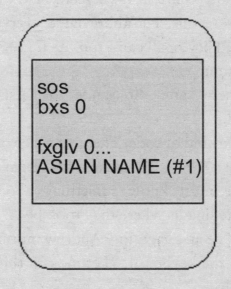

"What the —?" Andrew murmured. "SOS?"

"Mike must be in trouble," Evie said. "The Company must have figured out he's working for The Resistance."

"Bxs zero. That must mean there are no boxes. All the clues were taken."

Evie groaned. "Great. They have the maps. So they definitely know the location of Minotaur II!"

"Evie, this third line — fxglv zero. That's got to mean Foxglove. Mrs. Digitalis. Is he trying to tell us she's *dead*?"

"Or missing. Kidnapped."

"And what the heck does ASIAN NAME mean — after the Foxglove line?"

Evie squinted hard at the screen. "He was in a hurry when he wrote this. He abbreviated everything except these words. They're all caps, too. As if they're somehow more important."

"But there are thousands of Asian names," Andrew said.

"It's some kind of code. There's a space before the last two lines — it's like he means for them to be read together. He must know something about Foxglove. Maybe he's telling us where they took her."

"It could be an anagram," Andrew murmured, typing furiously on the keyboard. "Let me run this through an anagram website."

The screen instantly filled up with thousands of possibilities. "Too many," Evie said. "We have to narrow them down. Can we tell it to use only certain words — like, if he's giving us a location, he may be using the word *at* or *in*."

"There's an I and an N in ASIAN NAME..." Andrew moved his cursor down the computer screen, next to a line that said

INCLUDE THE FOLLOWING WORD IN ANAGRAM: _____

On the blank line, he typed

IN

In moments a list showed on the screen:

IN MANA SEA

IN ANA SAME

IN ANA AMES

IN ANA SEAM

IN ANA MESA

IN ANA AS ME

IN NASA MAE

IN MAE AN AS

IN SEA MA AN

IN SEA AM AN

IN A SEAMAN . . .

"Wait," Evie said. "Ana Mesa. Andrew, we know that name. It's some building — near school, I think."

"Have fingers, will Google." In seconds, Andrew was scrolling through a webpage jammed with text. "Okay. San Francisco public records. Ana Mesa Hotel. Here it is! '. . . abandoned by owner in 1994, fallen into disrepair . . . structural damage . . . condemnation delayed pending possible landmark designation.' This must be it, Evie! This is where they're holding Foxglove. We have to find her!"

"We? This is bigger than us, Andrew. *Way* bigger. We have to tell Mom. And Two." Evie sprang up from her chair and pulled open the door.

"You forgot to limp," Andrew said.

"It's only a sprain," Evie replied. Adrenaline, she realized, was an amazing thing. She hardly noticed the pain in her ankle.

They rushed down the hall to The Pit. Two was poring over a map on a table under the bank of monitors. "Excuse me, Ms. uh, Two," Andrew said. "But we heard from Mad Mike."

Two nodded impatiently. "Yes. He contacted us. SOS. Tried to continue but he was cut off."

"Our message said —" Andrew began.

But he was interrupted by a voice on the overhead monitor. "CCM2 . . . do you read me?"

It was a whisper, booming like the wind over the speakers. And it was totally familiar.

"*Mom*?" Andrew said.

He and Evie looked up to the big monitor. It showed an image of Andrew and Evie's street. It was dark, with pale circles of street lamp light on the pavement, but Evie could see the outline of their house over a hedge.

"What's she doing there?" Evie asked. "And how are we getting this image?"

"She's trying to get Mike," Two said with a sigh, shaking her head with either exasperation or admiration. "Your mother is amazing. We didn't want her to go. She's a code expert. Aboveground spying is not her thing. The Rogue Squad does that kind of stuff. But Mike happens to be both a Rogue and a Coder — unbelievably valuable to us. Unfortunately he's the *only* Rogue we have available right now. So your mother took it on herself to go after him. Her cell phone is sending us a video feed."

"But — but she —" Andrew began.

"Why didn't she tell us?" Evie demanded. "We're her *kids*. He's just a spy."

Mom's whispered voice, amplified, blotted out all sound in the room. "They're bringing him out of the house," she said.

A shadowy movement was barely visible in the dark image of the house's front door: the silhouette of two people carrying a third. Evie tried to make out faces, but it was too dark.

"He's breathing," Mom said. "The two goons are wearing masks. But the one on the left is —"

Her sentence ended in a grunt.

The image jittered and jerked. Then it went dead.

Chapter Five

Andrew ran. Down the tunnel, away from The Pit. Swinging his flashlight ahead of him, wrecking the evening for a small family of moles who skittered into a small hole on his left.

The Resistance could easily find him. He knew that. They could track him just as they'd tracked Pop. In a moment, he might hear the hidden doors closing.

But he heard nothing, and he knew why. Because The Resistance hadn't noticed he was gone yet. Because to them, Andrew and Evie were Spy X's cute kids, nothing more. The Resistance had huge problems now: Their secret was out, and two of their best people had been taken.

Taken. Mom had been *taken*.

The news had frozen him for a few moments. He had listened to all the shouting in The Pit — but most of it was about Problem 1: the security breach. The file uploads. The fact that, after the long battle, after all these years fighting The Company, the Resistance was losing.

Mom, it seemed, was Problem Number 2 — or 3. And there was much fretting about the lack of "Rogues."

Well, to Andrew, Mom was Number 1. No question. He'd lost her once. He wasn't going to let it happen again.

He couldn't let himself stand still. So he had just *left*. Without telling anyone. Not even Evie. With her ankle hurt, he had to go it alone. He'd start by going to the Ana Mesa and finding Foxglove. She'd help him find Mom. It was her specialty.

His breath echoed in the narrow, damp tunnel. He wouldn't have much time. Chaos or not, The Resistance would be too sharp not to notice his absence sooner or later. How much time did he have?

At the end of the corridor, the door was open — the one that had slid shut when they'd been running from Pop. That was a good sign. Maybe they'd reopened the entire system by now.

Andrew tried to recreate the path he'd taken.

Left out the door, and then left at the corner.

Andrew was tripping over the rough ground, splashing in the trickles of water. He was in the long passageway now, the one where Pop's flashlight had caught them in the glare. There had to be an opening to the right . . .

He swung the light around. It was the room where

they'd hidden from Pop. He ran through it, up an incline and into a narrow chamber . . .

BEEP BEEP BEEP BEEP BEEP BEEP BEEP!

The alarm rang out in the hallway, distant but echoing loudly.

They knew now.

Thump. Behind him, a door in the rock wall slid shut. He was trapped.

There. Ahead of him, rising straight up. The ladder he and Evie had used to descend into the tunnel. Above it was the Presidio — the area where Foxglove and the Franklins had rescued him.

Holding the flashlight in his teeth, he scrambled to the top.

The opening was shut solid. But there *had* to be a way of opening it. Some kind of emergency switch. The idea was to keep people out, not in.

He felt around. The ceiling was smooth.

Duh. The Resistance could control the branches of the maze. That meant they could control the exits, too. Would they block him from behind *and* from above?

He pounded the ceiling, but his fists bounced silently off the solid metal.

The flashlight, wet with saliva, slipped out of his

mouth. It fell to the ground with a dull *thwack*. The room went dark.

Great. Just great. What would he do now? He had some flash paper in his pocket, left over from a science experiment in school. That would set up a short, bright flare if he could light it. But what would he light it with?

Sweat stung his eyes. This whole escape attempt was stupid. Useless. What if he was stuck here? What if they closed off this chamber? It was a tiny room. How much air would he have?

"HELLLP! HELP MEEE!" he cried.

He heard a noise. A muffled bump. From above.

Then another. And another.

And slowly, above him, something began to move. With a rumbling metallic whine, a round section of the ceiling began to slide away.

A blast of cold air rushed into the chamber from above.

Two squinting brown eyes looked into his.

Andrew nearly lost his footing. "*Evie?*"

His sister reached down into the hole. "What would you do without me?"

He scrambled out into the park, falling onto the soft grass near an old cannon monument. "How did you get here?"

"Oh, you're welcome, don't mention it," Evie

drawled. "I saw you sneak away. And I wasn't going to let you go alone."

"But — but how did you get ahead of me? I didn't see you!"

"Number one, I can't run fast, so I couldn't follow you. Number two, I figured you'd try to retrace our long route. That is *so* inside the box, Andrew. Me? I used a shortcut. There's an exit near The Pit. Nice, too. An elevator. Anyway, *I* remembered seeing it on the map. They didn't notice me leaving. I came out in the Presidio, oh, fifty yards away — so I came straight here, figuring I'd find you. Just call me Rogue." Evie grinned. "Now come on, let's find Foxglove. She'll help us get Mom."

"That's just what I was thinking," Andrew said.

As Evie limped off into the woods, Andrew glanced around the area. His sister had rolled the three cannonballs onto three tree stumps, just the way the Franklins and Foxglove had done before to open the hatch.

Smart. Very smart. Sometimes he had to hand it to her.

Andrew followed her down a path through the woods. "It's confusing, but if we head this way, we'll reach Funston Avenue," Evie said. "That'll take us to Presidio Boulevard and onto Lombard, which will get us out of the park. From there, we're just a few blocks from the Ana Mesa, which is on Filbert and Broderick."

"How do you know all this?" Andrew asked.

Evie pulled a street map out of her back pocket. "I go low-tech sometimes. Now let's go!"

Evie had brought a flashlight of her own, and she shone it ahead of them as they walked. The night was still misty. A squirrel's rustle in the bushes made Andrew jump. His watch showed 3:17 A.M., which meant they'd been in Minotaur II for a little over three hours. It felt like ages.

The paved roads of the Presidio were empty streaks of solid black through the mist. Andrew and Evie kept to them carefully, reading street signs.

FOOOM!

The ground beneath them shook, and Andrew grabbed a tree. "What was that?"

"A five-point-seven on the Richter Scale, I'd say," Evie replied.

"An earthquake?" Andrew said. "It makes a noise like that?"

"Beats me. I've never been in one. Is it good or bad to be under trees?"

FOOOM!

The ground shook again.

"I don't feel safe here," Andrew said. "Can you go faster?"

"I'll try . . ."

As they crested a hill, a pinprick of light shone upward. Andrew breathed a sigh of relief. A streetlight from the neighborhood.

But the light moved quickly from side to side, catching Andrew full in the face.

It wasn't a streetlight. It was a flashlight.

Chapter Six

Evie pulled Andrew back into the woods. "Come on!"

"Wait," Andrew said. He hid behind a tree, listening for footsteps but hearing nothing. He waited a few moments, then carefully peeked around.

Someone was peeking back.

"Aggggh!" Andrew shouted.

"Shhhhh."

It was Mad Mike. His hair was messed up, his clothes dirty.

"Mike?" Evie blurted out. "Hey, we got your message — Ana Mesa!"

Mad Mike nodded enthusiastically. At the same time he put his finger to his mouth, shushing them. Then he reached into his pocket and pulled out two small sheets of paper. He gave one to Evie and one to Andrew. "Keep these," he whispered. "I can't talk. I'm being bugged. Everything I say is heard, every cell phone message is read. Don't know how they're doing it. You got my message?"

"Yes," Andrew said. "How did you get away? Did you find M —?"

Mad Mike shushed him again, pointing down toward town. He was telling them to leave, fast. As he backed away, toward Minotaur II, he opened his palm, closed it, and opened it again. Kind of a stiff good-bye gesture, Andrew thought. Sort of like Mr. Spock's Vulcan "Live Long and Prosper" — but without the split fingers.

Andrew waved back. But for some reason, Mad Mike's face fell. He looked upset.

He waved twice again and was out of sight.

Silently Andrew and Evie turned onto Presidio Boulevard and hurried downhill. "Did you see the look on his face?" Andrew asked. "Do you think he knows what's happening to The Resistance?"

"Sshh," Evie said.

The fog billowed up from the Bay as they emerged out of the Presidio. Filbert was two blocks south. The house windows were dark, and parked cars lined both sides of the street.

At the corner of Broderick stood a gabled building, its small front lawn filled with weeds. It was surrounded by a chain-link fence, and its windows were boarded over with planks of wood. A faded, hand-painted sign, ANA

MESA HOTEL, hung over the front door. Another that said VACANCY had fallen to the ground.

Andrew went to the gate, where a lock hung from a thick hasp. He took the lock in hand, looking up toward the hotel, checking for any movement, any sign of life.

"Hurry," Evie whispered.

Andrew reached into his pocket. He felt for the special key that he'd carried around ever since receiving it in a box Mom had sent.

The universal key, they called it. The key's round head was scored with ridges, like a quarter. Andrew dug his fingernail in and pulled downward. The ridges began to move around the circumference. The key's teeth retracted, making it thin and able to fit into the lock's keyhole. He inserted the key, then slowly turned the ridges the other way, until he heard a telltale *click*. A quick turn of the key, and the lock popped open.

Andrew slowly pushed the gate.

Screeeee. The gate was rusty. In the night's stillness, the squeak sounded like a tomcat.

He and Evie squeezed through an opening just wide enough for them to slip past. They tiptoed across a cracked, overgrown walkway.

"We could pry the wood off one of the windows," Evie whispered.

But Andrew had his eye on a basement entrance — slanted double doors at the side of the hotel. Putting his finger to his lips, he led Evie around the building. The double doors had been locked, too, but the hasp had rusted off its hinge and hung uselessly.

Carefully Andrew pulled on the handle, opening the door. A rush of stale, mildewed air came up from below.

And voices.

"She's not talking," one of them said.

"Give it up," another replied. "We've got orders to get the rat. Mike."

"And leave her here? Are you nuts?"

"Orders, pal. Their Mickey Mouse Club is self-destructing. We hit 'em now, we get 'em good. And it won't matter what she does or doesn't say. Come on."

Evie dug her fingers into Andrew's left arm. With his right, he quickly, silently closed the double doors.

They skittered toward the back of the building and hid behind a hulking Dumpster. "Did you recognize that voice?" Evie asked.

Before Andrew could answer, the cellar doors smacked open. He peeked around the Dumpster and saw the shadows of two people emerging. He did recognize one of them. The voice had been a giveaway, but the balding head confirmed it. He was known only as Spy N, and they'd met him in a tunnel under Alcatraz. He had tried to trap them. He'd lied, saying he was a colleague of Mom's. The sight of him stung. Andrew wanted to throw something at him. But he kept stock-still as Spy N and a stranger disappeared into the night.

"Andrew, they're going to —" Evie blurted out.

"Ssshh." Andrew took Evie by the arm, pulled her toward the double doors and yanked them open. They stared into a black hole. "They shut off the lights," he whispered. "You want to go first?"

"Andrew, we can't go down there!" Evie said, straining to look around the front of the house.

"If Mom's down there, Evie, we *have* to get her!"

A sudden soft *screeeee* sounded from the front of the house.

Evie gripped Andrew's arm. *"Andrew, we left the front gate open! They'll know we broke in!"*

With a loud clank, the gate slammed shut.

Chapter Seven

"What do we do now?" Evie whispered.

"Wait here," Andrew said. "And be ready to run."

He stepped away from the cellar doors and crept around the side of the house, keeping close to the wall. The raucous noise of crickets blotted out nearly all sound.

Carefully he peered across the front lawn. The gate was shut, the lock reattached.

Just beyond it, he heard the murmur of the two men's voices. "I didn't leave the gate open," one of them whined softly in the thick mist.

"Yeah, and you didn't let that kid Mike escape either, did you?" Spy N's voice replied sarcastically.

A car door slammed. Then another. An engine coughed to life and two headlights glared.

Andrew pulled back, sitting against the side of the house as the car drove away. He and Evie didn't dare breathe until the engine noise had died away.

Andrew peered down into the dark cellar. "Let's go before they come back."

"How do we know no one else is down there?" Evie asked.

"If you were a Company agent, would you wait in a cellar in total darkness?" Andrew said.

"I don't know!"

Andrew took Evie's flashlight and stepped onto the ladder. One rung. "We can't chicken out now," he said shakily.

He stepped down another rung, shining the flashlight downward. Cardboard boxes were strewn about. The walls held sagging shelves weighted down by tools and paint cans thick with dust. A blackboard rested against one wall, the words TONIGHT'S DINNER SPECIALS AT ANA MESA GRILLE printed across the top. Just beyond it, a stairway led upward into the building.

Across the dust-carpeted floor, a diagonal path looked like footprints in an early snow. Andrew stepped down with Evie close behind. The prints led to a long hallway, lined with numbered doors. There were two rows of them — 1 through 5 on one side, 6 through 10 on the other.

Storage rooms. Exactly like the ones they'd had when they lived in an apartment building in New York City.

Back then he thought they were apartments for monsters. They'd always terrified him.

So did these. Sort of.

Calling out to Foxglove was out of the question. Anyone upstairs would be able to hear him easily.

Tiptoeing closer, he noticed something odd about the storage room doors. A network of wires was strung along the moldings. He traced the path with his flashlight above each door, then down to a small sensor on each knob.

He shone the flashlight into his own face, turned to Evie, and mouthed the word *Alarm*.

No kidding, Evie mouthed back.

Now what?

Opening any one of these doors — maybe even just *touching* them — would trip an alarm. The Company would come running. Andrew and Evie would have to pick the right door, first time. No second chances. They'd have to unlock it, pull it open, get Mom, and bolt in a split second.

Evie was looking at him expectantly, impatiently.

Ba ba ba baaaaaaaa . . .

His cell phone's ring tone nearly made him hit the ceiling. Beethoven's Fifth. He fumbled for it in his pocket, quickly turning the sound off.

A text message appeared on the screen:

It's from Mike, Andrew mouthed.

fnd sps nu nfo. What did that mean?

Evie peered over his shoulder and into the lit screen. She quickly took a small notepad from her pocket, turned to a clean page, scribbled something, and held it under Andrew's flashlight.

FOUND SPIES - NEW INFO???

Andrew nodded. Maybe Mike had tracked down Spy N and his sidekick after they'd left the Ana Mesa. Maybe they drove into the Presidio.

Okay. There was a colon after *nu nfo*, which meant the info followed. And it was the old "bites in the donut" trick.

Mike must have gone through the Resistance code training. So he knew the trick. The problem was, Andrew didn't.

Somewhere in his pocket was the sheet where he'd copied down the donut dice codes from the program, back in Minotaur II. He fished around and came up with the crumpled-up sheet:

Evie took a corner and angled it so she could see.

It still made no sense. How were dice like donuts? How could they *possibly* figure it out in time?

It would have to wait.

No. It couldn't wait. What if it was crucial? What if Mike was telling them that Foxglove had been moved? Maybe it was a multilevel code: find the number and receive a priceless bit of information.

Andrew took a deep breath. Okay. Donuts.

Step one. Don't overthink it. That was Mom's instruction in an earlier message. Look at the elements. There had to be a pattern. Maybe something really simple. But what?

Evie suddenly jumped up. Her eyes bugged out and she grabbed a pencil out of her pocket.

On the bottom of Andrew's sheet, she wrote:

IT'S ONLY A DONUT IF IT HAS A HOLE!

Andrew stared at the words. Was on earth was she talking about?

Then he glanced at the dice again.

And he saw it.

A donut had a hole in the middle. Dice didn't, of course — but they had *dots* in the middle. Well, some of them did — the one, three, and five. The rest — the two, four, and six — did not.

Maybe the one, three, and five were *donuts*. On those

dice, and those dice only, the surrounding dots were *bites*!

Andrew glanced at the first example — the one they'd seen in the training program. The die at the end was a 1.

Was it a donut? Yes, because it had a hole in the center. But it had no bites. He took out his pencil and quickly wrote a zero on top of it.

To the left of that die was a 4.

Not a donut. No hole in the middle. So if it wasn't a donut, the other dots didn't count. Andrew wrote a zero on top of that, too.

Now he looked at the first die in the line. A 5.

It had a hole in the middle, so it was a donut — and it had four bites around the hole. So those four counted as bites!

He quickly finished the puzzle:

$$4 + O + 2 + O + O = 6!$$

 $= 6$

Evie nodded, grinning and clapping her hands silently.

Andrew quickly glanced at the other examples he'd copied down earlier. Yes. Every single one of them worked with this system.

What about the cell phone code?

Andrew scribbled the solution in no time. And he realized why Mike had looked frustrated when he'd waved good-bye so strangely.

Mike hadn't been waving. He'd been trying to tell

them something. He'd opened his palm once — twice. Five fingers. Then five fingers again.

$$2 + 0 + 4 + 0 + 4 = 10$$

Ten.

Andrew hadn't understood the gesture. So Mike had sent them this code.

Andrew and Evie both looked into the hallway.

To the door at the end of the hall marked 10.

Chapter Eight

Evie squeezed Andrew's hand.

This was it.

Foxglove had to be in there.

Andrew shone the flashlight on the door as they approached. They needed to act fast. The moment they broke the alarm circuit, they'd be in big trouble.

Evie's free hand shook as she reached for the doorknob. She turned it quickly and flung the door open.

Andrew braced for the alarm, but there was no sound.

The flashlight beam lit up a small, dingy space about six feet wide and eight feet deep. The walls were made of sheetrock and flecked with water stains. "Foxglove?" Evie whispered.

For a second they heard nothing.

And then, just inside the door, to the right: "Evie?"

Andrew barged into the room. Mom was standing against the wall, inches from the door. Waiting.

"*Mom?*" he said.

"No . . ." she murmured. "No! Why are you here?"

"We — we thought you'd be Foxglove," Andrew squeaked.

"*What are you doing out of Minotaur II?*"

Andrew expected Mom to be grateful, relieved, happy — any of the above — but not this.

Suddenly Mom stepped around them, lunging for the door.

Smack.

It slammed shut as her shoulder hit. She bounced back into the room, stumbling. Stunned, Andrew caught her in his arms.

In the hallway, on the other side of the door, voices hooted triumphantly. "*Hey*!" Evie shouted, banging on the door. "*Let us out!*"

"Did they hurt you, Mom?" Andrew asked.

"I'm fine," she replied, gathering them both in her arms. "And thank goodness you are, too. I didn't expect to see you here, guys. *You shouldn't be here. You put your lives in danger.*"

"We're only trying to help," Evie said.

She sighed heavily. "I know, sweetie. This is my fault. After all these months of staying incognito, I was stupid enough to do something I wasn't qualified to do and get myself captured. My pathetic attempt to be Rogue for a Day . . ."

"I thought we had it figured out," Andrew said, shaking his head in bewilderment. "How did they get us? I thought we ditched those guys."

"The Company had goons hiding in the dark," Mom replied. "When you saw Spy N and the other guy escape — that scene outside was staged. To lure you in here."

"This was a *trap*?" Evie asked.

Mom nodded. "I overheard them planning. They knew someone would come to find me. They saw that I came for Mad Mike, so they figured The Resistance would do the same for me. They didn't know it would be *you*, though. Well, neither did I." Mom gave them a weak smile. "Douse the flashlight, Andrew. Conserve the battery."

Andrew flicked the switch. "Mad Mike sent us a coded message about the Ana Mesa — before you were captured," he said. "There was something about Foxglove in the message, too."

"I don't know where she is, but it's not here," Mom said. "There must be several hiding places. Mike might have been confused. Chances are he heard the name Ana Mesa while he was spying at the house and got that info to you right away. Once we get out of here, I'll have to find her myself."

"Don't you mean, *we'll* have to find her ourselves?" Andrew asked.

Mom arched an eyebrow. "Don't press your luck."

"Mom, how did Mad Mike get away?" Evie asked.

"Oldest trick in the book," Mom said. "He played dead. They put us both in the backseat of a car. I knew he was conscious, because he slipped me a note. Anyway, when they brought us here, they set him down in Room 9. Well, I started fighting like crazy. He used the distraction to bolt. They were furious, of course — as you can imagine, they don't take kindly to double agents."

"So you *did* save him . . ." Evie said. "You left Minotaur II and risked your life for him."

"He's our best code person," Mom said. "He *thinks* codes, *dreams* codes. He can solve them and devise them faster than anyone I've seen."

"We saw him, too, Mom," Andrew said. "In the Presidio. Just a few minutes ago. He seemed to be heading back to Minotaur II. He says he's being bugged — everything he says, every message he sends on his cell. He gave us notes, too."

"The Company must have planted something on him when they thought he was unconscious. Their bugs are powerful and nearly undetectable. He'll find it, but it may take a while." Mom took the flashlight and flicked it on.

With her free hand, she reached into her pocket. "He's trying to tell us something. I can't make heads or tails of the note he gave me. Maybe if we put our three notes together."

She pulled out a piece of paper and held it to the light:

When the square spirals, begin with a shout that will prick up a horse's ear. Pull from the ground as you would kill a weed, and remember if the cow's in the corn, the _____ in the meadow. Abbreviated life stories will rub against the grain (but only that one which can be quick, rolled, or made into meal). End at a three-letter schl. in a salty four-letter state.

"Sheep's . . ." Andrew said.

"Sheeps?" Evie said.

"With an apostrophe," Andrew explained. "'The sheep's in the meadow, the cow's in the corn.' From the nursery rhyme. That's a start, at least . . ."

Andrew pulled his note out and unfolded it:

When staying strictly in the shade, a scientific premise precedes that which in Yemen is a German van.

"*Whaaaat*?" Andrew said.

"Mine is just as bad," Evie replied, holding hers out for the others to see:

In areas of light between dark is the bill used between Mediterranean and Baltic, the time occurring between Aug and Oct, and the plunder split between pirates.

"*September*!" Andrew said. "The time between August and October. That's two clues. Do you think these codes are a key to our escape?"

"I don't think so," Mom said. "He had written my note before we got here. He probably wrote it inside the house before he was caught. Possibly the other notes, too. Maybe he had discovered some important information and wanted to split it into three parts. For security. This could be about where The Company hid the clues from your closet, or where they took Foxglove."

" 'A square that spirals'?" Andrew said. "What does that mean?"

Mom examined the three sheets carefully. "My hunch is that something is missing from this code. The first part of each note is significant . . . a square that spirals, strictly in the shade, light between dark . . . it's some kind of key. I think it could be referring to something we don't have yet. Let's get out of here first, before we try to solve this. Hold on to the notes. When we have some light and some time, we'll work on them again. I assume you're good at this by now."

"We figured out the donut code," Evie said proudly, putting the three notes in her pocket.

"Some people never get that one," Mom said. "Well, we'll have to continue your training — if we can ever recover the program, that is."

"Mom, what's going to happen to The Resistance?" Andrew asked. "When we left, they were uploading data. Where was it going?"

Mom lifted her free arm and directed the flashlight to the inside of her bicep. "You can see it . . . barely. They did a terrible job embedding. It was a long time ago and they've gotten better at it since. They don't usually use the arm. But it's in there."

Andrew and Evie leaned forward, straining to see. A scar ran diagonally across her arm. Under it was a slight whitish discoloration. Andrew remembered noticing it when he was little.

"A bike accident," he said. "That's what you told me it was."

"It's a chip," Mom said. "An extremely high-capacity

memory chip with broadband receiver capability. That's where the data went. Part of The Resistance's data and system files are inside me, and inside Foxglove and the Franklins and many others."

"So The Resistance is portable," Andrew said. "It's being carried around until you guys find another head-quarters."

"Exactly," Mom replied. "We weren't sure we'd have to do something this drastic. We were hoping it would be enough to close off branches of the tunnel system, maybe even collapse them. You probably felt that rumble a few minutes ago. There will be more of them. Possibly the whole system, I'm afraid. Now that Pop found the map of Minotaur II, all bets are off."

"*Pop* found it?" Andrew said. "Not Marisol? How do you know?"

"If Pop found the map, there's hope," Evie added. "He wouldn't put our lives in danger."

Mom sighed deeply. "Evie, when your father leaves for work, does he ever tell you exactly where he's going or who he works for?"

"Of course not," Andrew said. "You know the drill. He could tell us, but he'd have to shoot us? You both said the same thing. Pop was in covert operations. You were in international business. That was all we knew."

"But by now, I'm sure he's told you a little more," Mom said, measuring her words. "That I betrayed The Company. That I couldn't be trusted."

Andrew glanced at his sister. *How did Mom know?* "Sort of," he replied.

"Well, then, in the interest of fair disclosure, he should have mentioned his employer," Mom said. "Or that he's known at work by the name Company Agent MO22072619. Internal Operations."

"Pop works for The Company?" Evie asked.

No. I am not hearing this. Andrew shook his head, as if by doing so he could somehow dislodge the thought and make it go away. "No. No — he has contacts with them," Andrew murmured. "But he doesn't know. He *can't* know."

"I know this is hard to hear," Mom said steadily, "but Richard has been a Company loyalist since day one. A true believer. That, more than anything else, was the reason I had to go into hiding."

"So, when he was with Marisol in the tunnel, he was working *with* her?" Andrew asked.

"Back when you were finding out bad stuff about The Company," Evie said, "did you *show* Pop what you'd found? He would have understood. I mean, *you* were a Company loyalist once, too, right?"

"We were both Company members when we met," Mom said sadly. "Weddings between members were encouraged. The Company is very sly. They know you have spying in your blood. And they expect you to spy on each other. To do their work for them."

"He married you *to spy on you*?" Andrew said.

Mom shook her head. "No. I don't think Pop had any bad intentions at first. But when I started finding out the truth about The Company — their rise to power during the Cold War, the way they'd silenced critics — things changed. I saw his name on documents. He had signed off on certain expenses — weapons, infiltration devices. I thought his signature had been forged or that he hadn't known what he was doing. I didn't want to *believe* he knew. I tried to draw him out, but he'd get defensive. So I dug deeper. I learned that The Company knew their secrets were being leaked. They were in spin mode, spreading rumors that The Resistance was a group of anti-American subversives — failed Company spies now bent on revenge. They said The Resistance had to be destroyed in the name of national security. Meanwhile, they'd decided the U. S. government was too permissive, too incompetent. They stopped wanting to help the administration. They began to believe they could take over and do a better job."

"Like a dictatorship," Andrew said.

"Maybe, maybe not," Mom said. "I never found out how they plan to run things. But our system is not built to resist the kind of takeover they're plotting. They've been working from within — corporations, government agencies, lobbying groups. They're amassing huge sums of money. And they're willing to wait as long as it takes until they build up a force strong enough to succeed."

"Pop is too smart to fall for something like that," Andrew said.

"It takes a *lot* to fool a smart person into thinking black is white," Mom replied. "But when it happens, you have the strongest convert imaginable. When people have been convinced they're part of a revolution, sometimes they lose their capacity to reason."

"He isn't a *convert*," Evie said. "He's your husband. And our father."

Mom didn't answer for a long time. When she spoke, her voice was barely audible. "You're right on the first count. He is my husband."

It was not the answer Andrew had expected. Her silence was the loudest thing in the room. "You mean, he's not our —"

"Oh, Mom . . ." Evie murmured.

"Your father passed away when you were babies,"

Mom said softly. "He was the kindest, strongest man I knew. I never thought I'd fall in love again, until I met Richard."

Andrew's mind raced. Pop was their stepfather, not their father. It didn't seem possible. "How come you never told us?"

"I always wanted to," Mom replied, "always planned to, but —"

The sound of loud footsteps silenced her. She pulled Andrew and Evie back into a corner of the room.

A key turned in the door. Slowly it opened.

Click.

A light blinked on, revealing a figure in the doorway. Andrew felt his heart jump. "You . . ." he said.

Chapter Nine

"Kids . . . ?"

There he was, and for a nanosecond the last conversation had vanished, the last *ten months* had vanished, and they were home in their Connecticut living room, playing a game of Boggle. Pop had just returned from a hard day's work. In a moment Andrew and Evie would run to him, spilling over with the day's news from school. Then off to the kitchen they'd go, to make dinner or to smell whatever was already cooking.

It was a fantasy. A stupid fantasy.

Once upon a time, fantasies made Andrew feel better. But the biggest one of his life had just exploded. In his mind's story, the Finding of Mom had an ending like a video game. Triumph and shouting. Mission accomplished. Nightmare over. Pop and Mom hug and kiss, Andrew and Evie high-five. Life goes back to normal. Maybe even some swelling music.

But Andrew knew better now. Fantasies hurt. They hurt hard and deep. They lifted you up to places that you could never reach, then they let you down with a crash. The only thing that mattered was reality. And the reality was that they were in the basement storage room of a stinky, boarded-up hotel, facing a man who had fooled them into thinking he was their father. And he was here to betray them, not make them dinner.

"Hey, big guy," Pop said. "It's only me. Evie? Cassie? Let me see you."

Pop hung a lantern on a hook in the wall, and for the first time Andrew could see everyone's face. Mom, looking wary. Evie, pale.

Pop was alone. His face was lined and haggard-looking. He seemed so much older. Andrew found himself examining Pop's features, the shape of his face, trying to determine if there was a resemblance. There had to be a resemblance.

"It's been a long time, Richard," Mom said with a reluctant cheerfulness. "I have to say, it looks like you took good care of the kids. Well, Andrew does need a haircut . . ."

"I do?" Andrew said.

Pop smiled and tousled Andrew's hair. Andrew cringed. Then he cringed again, because he hated himself for cringing.

But he couldn't help it. It felt like the twist ending of

The Sixth Sense, where the thing you learn in the final second changes everything that has happened before.

Bruce Willis is really a ghost.

Your father is not really your father.

Suddenly he was seeing Pop's face through different eyes. The long, thin nose, with two small bumps on either side. The wide forehead, the cleft in the chin, the square jaw. The pale skin that burned so easily in the sun. *None of them*, Andrew thought. *I have none of them.*

People were always saying to Andrew's friends, *You look just like your dad*. But did they ever say it to Andrew? Hardly ever. Why had he never noticed that? Did other people know the truth? Were Andrew and Evie the last to find out?

The stepfather part — that didn't really matter. Andrew knew plenty of kids with stepfathers or divorced fathers or no fathers. Having a stepfather wasn't a bad thing. But the lie mattered. A lot. And as Pop himself had often said, one lie leads to another.

At that moment, Andrew felt smothered by lies.

Evie finally spoke up. "Mom says you're the enemy, Pop —"

"That's a misunderstanding, sweetie," Pop said. "I'm sure we can —"

"— And that you're not our father," Evie barged on.

The words caught in Pop's throat. His calm, take-charge, *Pop* expression weakened, and he cast a bewildered glance at Mom.

"I told them, Richard," Mom said. "They had to find out sooner or later. It should have happened long ago."

Pop's face slowly sank. "Well. Wow. I . . . I suppose I was waiting for the right moment to tell you the truth and I never found it. Mom's right. I should have. You guys were way old enough. I guess I'm a weak man that way."

"We wouldn't have cared, Pop," Evie said. "We wouldn't have stopped liking you just because you're not . . ." Her voice drifted off.

"Not what?" Pop asked. "Not your father? Tell me, Evie, do you remember the fellow who gave you your life — that wonderful man, may he rest in peace? Andrew — how about you? Can you picture him?"

Evie and Andrew both clammed up.

"That's unfair, Richard," Mom said. "They were babies."

"I know," Pop said gently. "But tell me, then, what does father *mean*? Who can claim that title? What do you call the only guy you *do* remember — the one who shared your earliest memories? Who fed you, cared for you, took you to the doctor, bought you clothing, all that stuff?"

"Richard, please," Mom said.

"Are you one of them, Pop?" Evie said. "Are you a Company agent? Do you want to overthrow the government?"

Pop let out a bewildered laugh. Then a louder, angrier one. "Is that what you've been told? Yes, I work for The Company. But The Company is *part* of the government. If I overthrew it . . . well, that's preposterous. I'd lose my job. Where would the paycheck come from?"

"You're not being straight with them, Richard," Mom said, her face reddening even in the dim glow of the lantern.

"Cassandra," Pop replied, "you can take away my claim to fatherhood — granted, I was asking for something I didn't fully deserve. But you cannot take away my integrity."

"You lost that already," Mom said, nearly spitting the words. "When you signed your soul over to The Company."

Evie suddenly lurched across the floor. Pop flinched, and for a moment Andrew thought she was going to attack him. Instead she flung her arms around his waist and hugged him hard, sniffling. "I — I'm sorry. I don't know who to believe anymore. But, Pop . . . you've always been my father. Don't be sad."

Andrew glanced at Mom. She had retreated to the corner of the room, her face a blank.

He didn't know how to feel. "What about Marisol, Pop?" he asked. "She tried to hurt Evie. And that other guy — Spy N —"

"Spy N is a low-level functionary," Pop said. "After what he did to you, he'll be demoted. And Marisol? Well, she's a trainee. Youthful and overzealous. But, she hurt you? I wish you'd said something."

"We were supposed to keep everything secret," Evie said.

Pop glared at Mom. "I know how hard these last ten months have been, Evie and Andrew," he said softly. "You needed a parent, and I tried to do the work of two."

"If I hadn't left, they wouldn't have a mother!" Mom blurted out. "You drove me away, Richard. And now you've broken the back of The Resistance. You got me and the kids where The Company wants us. I know what they want. Why don't you just let them take us? Why are you here? How can you say these things to your own kids with a straight face?"

"I beg your pardon?" Pop said, drawing Evie tighter. "I thought they *weren't* my kids, Cassie, only yours. Isn't that what you've been telling them?"

"Not exactly, Pop," Andrew said.

"I was hoping I could talk to you, Cassie," Pop went on. "It's not the Cold War anymore. You uncovered some old Company secrets, things from the distant past. The Company has changed. The government needs us now more than ever. The Resistance is helping no one, draining our resources — it's a relic of the seventies. And somehow it managed to steal you from us. I was hoping I could reach you . . ."

"Pop, you're holding me too tight," Evie said. "That hurts."

"*Let go of her.*" Mom's voice was low and tense, like a tight string about to break.

"Frankly, Cassie, after what you've done and who you've been associating with," Pop said, "I'm not sure it's in the best interest of the kids to be with you. I'm afraid I'll have to take them back. And I think you'd benefit from seeing a counselor over at Company headquarters."

"Over my dead body!"

Andrew couldn't take it anymore. "Stop!" he said. "*Will you two stop?*"

His voice was quickly swallowed up in the small room.

"I'm offering all of you a chance," Pop said. "Come with me. You'll be my responsibility."

"And if we don't go?" Andrew asked.

"You can stay and wait for them without me," Pop replied.

"*Them*?" Andrew said.

"I'll take my chances," Mom said.

Pop exhaled deeply. "Fine. Let's let the children decide for themselves."

Andrew felt pinned to the spot. He watched the resolve in Mom's face crack. What was going to happen when Pop left? What would The Company do to her? Would they let her go? And if they did, where would she go? Was there still a Resistance?

Pop was giving him and Evie an invitation to freedom. It seemed stupid to say no. But Mom wasn't stupid. And Mom didn't lie.

Long ago, Mom had taught them what to do in an impossible decision. You drew a line down the middle of a sheet of paper. Then you listed the pros on one side and the cons on the other. The side that had the longest list won.

Andrew tried to imagine two sheets — one for The Resistance and one for The Company. In his mind he drew a line down both. He thought of Marisol and Foxglove and Alcatraz and the Franklins and Spy N and Mad Mike and Mom's boxes and the fake boxes and the truth of Pop's identity and the people he'd met in Minotaur II. He watched each item hop into its place under Pro and Con until the sheets filled up.

And he knew where he stood.

Slowly Pop unhooked his lantern from the wall. He shone it one last time into the room and turned.

Evie hesitated, glancing from Mom to Andrew. Then, choking back a sob or a question, Andrew wasn't sure which, she and Pop walked out.

Andrew looked at Mom. The door closed behind Pop and Evie. And a lock made a sharp *click*.

Chapter Ten

Evie was only vaguely aware of the odd quietness of the San Francisco streets. As her dad steered his Ford Freestyle over the hills, her mind was racing.

Was she doing the right thing?

Evie didn't know. She wasn't sure she could know.

She didn't feel much right now except stunned.

The thing was, she thought Mom and Andrew would be right behind her. It seemed like a no-brainer. Stay in the claustrophobic room — *don't* stay in the claustrophobic room. Cut off Pop completely — continue the conversation with Pop in the fresh air. Pop had sounded reasonable. Was he telling the truth? Maybe he was, maybe not. Maybe he thought he was — and maybe Mom thought she was, too. That kind of thing happened. Still, reasonable people *talked*, right? Okay, Mom had said "Over my dead body" — but how could she have meant it? How could she have wanted to stay there?

She wasn't in her right mind, that's why. Pop had

made her so angry. Evie had never heard her voice like that. Pop should have realized she needed more time.

If only he'd given her and Andrew a few more minutes . . .

"Why did you lock the door like that?" Evie asked. "Maybe they would have come."

Pop shook his head sadly. "I know your mom. She wasn't going to move. And I could see in Andrew's eyes that he would do whatever she did."

"But leaving them in that dump? That's not like you, Pop."

"Oh, dear — oh, you thought —?" Pop let out a chuckle. "They're not *staying* there, sweetie. Spy F had instructions to take them upstairs, give them some food, ask them a few harmless questions, and then let them go."

"So we'll see them at home?" Evie asked.

At the top of a hill, Pop signaled left where he was supposed to signal right. "Unfortunately our house is a disaster area, Evie. A total mess. We'll go to one of The Company's safe houses. It's a former YMCA. You can get some rest there."

"Disaster area? There wasn't that much stuff for them to dig up. It was all in Andrew's closet. Did you see it?"

Pop sighed. "I'm afraid some of The Company members can be a little energetic in their search techniques. And yes, I was there. I did see it. Codes, secret messages, spy gizmos. Typical Resistance nonsense, Evie. You know who they are? Frustrated cryptographic experts with nothing better to do than send kids on wild goose chases and spread rumors of civil war."

"Mom sent us that stuff, Pop."

"How do you know it was her, Evie? How do you know someone wasn't doing it in her name?"

Evie didn't have an answer for that. But the thought of their house brought back the image of Mad Mike being carried out the front door. Of Mom being abducted out front. Of Foxglove's disappearance.

"Pop, when you were at the house . . ." Evie let her voice drift off.

The notes. Mad Mike's notes.

She felt for them in her pocket. They were still there.

He'd been trying to tell them something. But some crucial element was missing to tie the notes together. For a moment Evie thought she might mention this to Pop.

No. Mike was a double agent. Pop worked for The Company. Mentioning the notes could get Mike in big trouble.

She vowed to herself to look at them again, though. When she was safe in a bedroom.

"Yes?" Pop said.

"What?" Evie replied.

Pop laughed. "You started to ask me a question. 'When you were at the house . . .'"

"Nothing," Evie said. "Just daydreaming, I guess."

Pop stopped for a red light. They were at the top of a hill now, near the Mark Hopkins Hotel, looking down on a spectacular view of the valley. It was an amazing neighborhood. "When we're all together," Evie said, "we'll need a bigger house."

"Don't give up hope, Evie," Pop said, smiling. "They'll come around."

After a few blocks Evie felt the tires bump over the cable car tracks. Soon the neighborhood started looking more rundown.

He pulled up to the curb in front of a dark, imposing granite building with stocky pillars. "Where are you taking me?" she asked.

"I'm afraid I have some urgent work to do, so I'm leaving you with Ms. Austin. You'll like her."

Evie climbed out of the car. The street was desolate, save for a lone shabby figure huddled under a mostly collapsed cardboard box next door. A pair of eyes peered out of the box.

Instinctively Evie reached for Pop's hand.

He seemed momentarily startled, but he relaxed when he saw the homeless man. With a friendly smile, he waved. "That's Nails. As in 'hard as nails.' Marksman, Rhodes scholar. We signed him right out of Oxford. Yale before that. No one gets past him."

"He's in disguise?" Evie asked. "A guy like that, doing security?"

"People are dying to work for us and, for him, it's a start," Pop said.

He put a magnetic card into a slot and pushed open a thick glass door covered with ancient CLOSED signs. Just inside was a vaulted lobby, lit only by a strip of dim fluorescent lights. In the center was a high marble desk and chair that looked as if they hadn't been used in years.

A movement in the shadows made Evie jump.

Slowly, an old woman in a rumpled blue uniform sidestepped into the light, pushing a mop across the floor. "Hello, Yohanna," Pop said.

As the woman turned, Evie realized she wasn't old at all. Her lipstick, a bright shade of blush red, was the only real color in the dreary room. "Velcome back," she said in a deep-throated European-accented voice. "You found your family?"

"Just one of them," Pop said. "We'll get the others later. Evie Wall, meet Yohanna Austin. She'll take care of you. Ms. Austin, make sure Evie gets a comfortable room. She needs lots of sleep."

"Charmed," said Ms. Austin, extending a hand. Her wrist was thin and dainty, her nails painted in a blue-silver diagonal design. Suddenly the shabby uniform seemed fashionable and elegant. Just shaking her hand made Evie feel like a doofus. "You vill zleep on a zoft and downy bett — like de sheeps."

"Sheeps?" Evie said nervously.

Pop gave Evie a quick kiss and scurried down a dark corridor.

Silently Ms. Austin offered Evie her elbow. Together they walked through the lobby. Ms. Austin looked straight ahead, not saying a word. Her heels clopped steadily on the old marble tile as she led Evie into a tiny office cluttered with file cabinets, papers, clothing, cleaning supplies, and piles of photos. "I am an amateur photographer," Ms. Austin explained with a smile. "Alzo a ferry messy person."

She put the mop against a desk and took Evie back

out into the lobby, to an old elevator with a battered metal door. She pressed a button and a loud machine began to whine.

Evie felt tongue-tied. Ms. Austin made her nervous. Who was she anyway — and why did she talk like that, all those odd words and pronunciations?

Like *sheeps*. That's what she'd said. Not *sheep*.

Sheeps just happened to be one of the clues in Mom's note. A weird coincidence or what?

As the elevator door opened, Ms. Austin gestured for Evie to enter. "You haff nussing to vorry about," she said with a wink. "Zorry iff I zpeak vit too shtrong an accent. I am von Germany."

Germany. There was something about Germany in Andrew's clue. Another coincidence?

Easy, Evie. You're on edge. Get it together.

She stepped onto the elevator. The cab was an old accordion-wall steel cage that Ms. Austin operated with a hand crank. They rode it up to the third floor, where it opened onto a drab hallway of yellowing tiles.

At the end of the long hallway was a plastic sign that pointed left for LODGING and right for YOUTH.

"Links," said Ms. Austin. "I mean, left, pleass. Vhere it zess Lotchink." Evie turned down the hall and Ms. Austin opened the door to Room 7.

It was a tiny hotel-style bedroom with a sink, a dresser, a night stand, and a lamp. The bed had been made and turned back nicely.

Evie flopped onto the bed. It felt heavenly. "Mmmm. Thank you." As Evie moved her feet under the covers, her toes touched a small sheet of paper. She went to reach for it, but something told her to stop.

Ms. Austin smiled and gave her a wink. "Ve vill zpeak zoon," she said. "Ees oatmeal okay for your breakfast tomorrow?"

"Fine," Evie replied. "Good night."

"Sveet dreams," Ms. Austin said.

The door shut. Evie waited for the sound of footsteps to retreat.

A strange animal sound — like the yelp of a fox — came from the alley outside.

The fox went out on a stormy night, Evie thought. *Prayed for the moon to give him light*. The first line of a song she sang in summer camp.

Evie glanced outside. A sliver of moonlight angled across the alley. She saw Mad Mike's face for a moment, looking up, before he disappeared into the shadows.

Then she quickly pulled out the sheet of paper and held it under the lamplight.

"What the —?" she muttered to herself.

That which goes out on a stormy night must protect its hands against the cold.

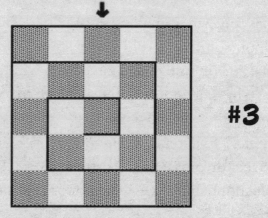

#3

Chapter Eleven

"They're snoring," Andrew whispered, his ear touching the door.

The Company goons had taken his cell phone. That was it. Not much drama. No torture or threats or cackling in strange languages. Not even any questioning, really. In fact, the two guys were sort of mild and ordinary-looking. They could have been the local grocers.

Mom stood in the corner, shining the flashlight on a pile of folded-up newspapers. "I'm still not sure this is a good plan," she said. "It's risky."

"It's all we've got," Andrew replied. "And risk is my middle name."

Mom arched an eyebrow at him. With a deep breath, she unscrewed the glass top of the light so that the bulb was exposed. In her left hand, she held a silvery strip of paper — Andrew's flash paper. "Okay, pal, let's roll."

Andrew began coughing violently.

"Andrew?" Mom shouted. *"Baby, are you all right? HELP! IT'S MY SON'S ASTHMA!"*

Andrew heard a commotion in the hallway and nodded to Mom. She touched the tip of the bulb to the silvery paper, and it flared.

The pile of newspapers went up instantly.

Andrew and Mom both sank to the floor, Andrew to the right of the door and Mom to the left. Smoke was quickly spreading.

They'd have only a few moments.

The shouting in the hallway became louder. Keys rattled and fell to the floor.

A moment later the door burst open, and the two men rushed in. Shouting, coughing, cursing, they went right to the far corner and began stamping out the fire.

Andrew and Mom sprang for the door. Andrew quickly shut it behind them, then pulled open the hinged door of a metal box on the wall. Inside was a line of switches. He flicked one marked ALARM SYSTEM from OFF to ON.

"Hurry," he urged, rushing across the cellar floor. But instead of heading outside, Mom pulled Andrew under the wooden stairs.

"Why are we staying here?" Andrew asked.

"Precaution," Mom said. "Get ready to run."

Smoke was starting to waft out from the storage rooms. The door to number 10 flew open.

Andrew put his fingers in his ears.

Waaaa . . . Waaaa . . . Waaaa . . .

The alarm was deafening. The two goons, doubled over and coughing, stumbled out of the room. Smoke billowed into the cellar.

Smack!

The outside door smashed open, directly over Andrew and Mom. Footsteps raced downward. Andrew counted one person, two, three . . . In moments, five people were in the cellar, all shouting at each other.

"I think that's all of them," Mom whispered. "Cover your mouth and nose!" She grabbed Andrew's hand, darted out from under the stairs, and scrambled for the door.

The fresh night air felt like a long, cool drink of water as they raced outside, around the house, and toward the gate. "Andrew, your key!" Mom cried.

Andrew dug in his pocket for the universal key and gave it to her.

"Where are they?" a voice shouted from behind them.

"Hurry!" Andrew urged.

Chink.

The lock fell open. Mom pushed the squeaky gate. Behind them, the voices grew louder as they slipped out and ran to the right.

At the corner, Mom stopped at a parked late-model Oldsmobile. "This is one of theirs."

"Spies drive Oldsmobiles?" Andrew said.

Using the universal key, Mom quickly unlocked the doors. As Andrew jumped inside, Mom worked the ignition.

Vrroommm!

"You're quick," Andrew said.

"Your plan got us out of there," Mom said with a smile. "What other kid carries around flash paper?"

She floored the accelerator. With a screech of tires, the car flew away from the curb.

They drove away into the night, the shouts fading as they reached Lombard Street.

"Where to now?" Andrew asked.

"Downtown San Francisco," Mom said. "We've tracked The Company to several locations, all clustered around their system of tunnels. The locations aren't all reliable. Some of them are real, some are decoys — abandoned buildings, old YMCAs that no self-respecting Company spy would ever set foot in. So it'll be a little like finding a needle in a haystack. Well, maybe something bigger than that."

"A light saber in a haystack?"

"Exactly. Trouble is, I know our list of locations

isn't complete — for example, we didn't know about Ana Mesa."

"So we're just going to *all* of them?"

Mom turned on Broadway, heading straight for downtown. "Before daybreak, we'll find the right one — with Pop and your sister inside."

Andrew stared out the window as the streets of San Francisco raced by, still lit up despite the hour.

Chapter Twelve

Under her nighttable lamp, Evie carefully laid out the three sheets Mad Mike had given to her, Andrew, and Mom. Next to them she unfolded a fourth sheet — the one she'd found under her bedcovers, which contained the strange shape and message.

The first sentence on Mom's sheet jumped out at her:

When the square spirals, begin with a shout that will prick up a horse's ear.

Then she glanced at the shape in the fourth sheet.

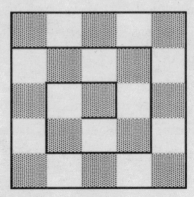

Yes. A spiraling square!

The messages had to be related to the shape. It appeared to be some kind of weird crossword puzzle. But crosswords contained *numbers* for the UP and DOWN words — and numbered clues to match. This had neither. By now, she and Andrew had seen some strange crossword puzzles, but nothing like this.

She scanned the three sheets of paper. The sentences contained the clues, somehow. She'd have to decode those clues. Then she'd have to figure out how they fit.

BEGIN WITH A SHOUT THAT WILL PRICK UP A HORSE'S EAR.

Okay. The logical place to begin was the upper left corner. The squares seemed to start there and spiral inward. Or did they start in the center and spiral outward?

Left to right made the most sense.

Evie exhaled. At times like this, she wished she were a country girl. You yelled "Soooeee" to a pig, or something like that. What did you yell to a horse? "Giddyup"? "Whoa"? "Word up"? "Hey, you"?

Hey.

That was it. A play on words. If you shouted *hey*, a horse would assume it was *hay* and listen up. A shout that will prick up a horse's ear.

She carefully wrote the word into the grid:

Okay. Next: PULL FROM THE GROUND AS YOU WOULD KILL A WEED.

That could be *yank* or *jerk* or a number of other things.

REMEMBER IF THE COW'S IN THE CORN, THE _____ IN THE MEADOW.

She knew that one already — *sheep's* (or *sheeps*). But she couldn't fill that in without knowing how long the previous word was.

ABBREVIATED LIFE STORIES WILL RUB AGAINST THE GRAIN (BUT ONLY THAT ONE WHICH CAN BE QUICK, ROLLED, OR MADE INTO MEAL). END AT A THREE-LETTER SCHL. IN A SALTY FOUR-LETTER STATE.

Ugh. How many clues *were* there?

Evie's eyes traveled wearily around the spiral. The last clue was three letters long. It would fit in the last three letters in the puzzle. SCHL. — that would be school. SALTY FOUR-LETTER STATE — that could be state as in United States. Iowa . . . Utah . . . Ohio. Or it could mean a four-letter state of mind.

Like weak. Beat. Sunk.

Suddenly she could think only in four-letter words. It was *late*. And she couldn't stifle a *yawn*.

This was *hard*. Too hard. She scanned the other two sheets, trying to figure out anything. But when she reached the part about the German van in Yemen, she gave up. Evie hated to admit it, but she needed Andrew. He was a great code partner.

She wondered how her brother was doing. Pop had promised that Andrew and Mom would be taken care of. Were they sleeping in a bedroom like this? Were they answering questions in Room 10 at the Ana Mesa? Were they as tired as she felt?

She flopped back on the bed and closed her eyes. The last thing she saw before dozing off was a flock of sheep, leaping in a meadow in Iowa.

Chapter Thirteen

"Oh my God . . ." Mom muttered, staring into the rearview mirror.

Andrew turned to see flashing blue lights on the unmarked car behind them. Mom had been driving fast. Too fast. But who would have expected cops to be patrolling for speeders at this hour?

Andrew ducked. "Outgun them, Mom!"

But she was already slowing, steering onto the side of the road. "I cherish our lives too much to get into a car chase," she said. "I'll talk to them."

"*Talk to them?* It's a stolen car, Mom! They'll put you in jail."

"Reach in the glove compartment, Andrew. See if you can find a registration. We'll say it's your uncle's car. At this time of the night, they're looking for hard-core criminals. With a mother and son, I'm hoping they'll go easy."

"If not?"

"We'll cross that bridge when we come to it."

Great. Just great. They escape an evil secret spy ring bent on national domination, only to be stopped for speeding.

Mom rolled down the window and turned off the engine. Andrew heard footsteps crunching on the gravel. A flashlight's beam caught Mom in the face. Squinting, she forced a smile. "What can I do for you, Officer?" she asked.

A dozen different rescue scenarios flashed through Andrew's mind. He could pretend to be deathly sick, throw open the back door into the cop's solar plexus, jump up and yell "boo," frightening the cop so that Mom could take off.

A gruff voice replied, "You're under arrest for disappearance from society for ten months, including a missed-eleventh-birthday violation."

Mom's jaw dropped.

Andrew looked up. He saw a pot belly and tattooed arm.

"Gotcha — haw, haw, haw!" a familiar voice bellowed, followed by a woman's raucous, high-pitched laugh.

Andrew sat up. "Mr. and Mrs. Franklin?"

Mrs. Franklin, dressed in her usual hippie-biker black

leather, gave him a maternal wink. Her husband was laughing so hard he was beginning to wheeze. "We fooled 'em, Eulalia!" he squawked.

"You're good, Sedgewick," Mom said, her face turning red with embarrassment. "Too good."

Andrew had never been more relieved in his life. The Franklins were Resistance members whose daughter, Doreen, was in his and Evie's grade. Mr. and Mrs. Franklin, along with Foxglove, had helped the twins find Mom and Minotaur II.

"How did you find us?" Andrew asked.

"There's a skeleton crew still in Minotaur II," Mrs. Franklin said. "They told us you'd escaped. We were looking without much luck, until you got into this car."

"I've been planting tracers on Company cars for the last five months," Mr. Franklin explained. "When Two got the signal that this car was on the move, we jumped. I told Eulalia it would be you, trying to escape, but she didn't believe me."

"We're going to check out some Company sites," Andrew explained.

"They have Evie," Mom went on. "Richard took her."

"I know," Mr. Franklin said solemnly. "Do you have a cell phone?"

"They took our phones away," Mom said.

Mr. Franklin pulled a small phone and sheet of paper from his pocket and handed them to Mom. "Eulalia and I will tell CCM2 to cut off transmission to your phones — so The Company doesn't pick up messages meant for you. Meanwhile, you can take one of ours. Go to the address on this sheet. I'm not sure what's there. Mad Mike sent it to us, and so far he's been our best source. He's in the field right now, but they're on his tail, so he can't stay in one place very long. Don't expect to see him."

"Thanks," Mom said. "I owe you one."

Mr. Franklin grinned. Backing away from the curb, he touched the brim of his black leather cap. "Just stay under the speed limit, ma'am."

Mom gunned the accelerator and headed downtown.

Moments later, she was turning onto a dark street and cutting the lights. She glided to a stop at the curb. "This is it," she said, peering at Mr. Franklin's note.

Andrew glanced out the window. It wasn't exactly a welcoming neighborhood. The street was lined with empty lots and buildings protected by roll-down metal gates. Just beyond them was a square six-story building with thick pillars flanking the entrance. It was dark except for a few dimly lit upper-floor windows.

Mom quietly opened her door and stepped out.

Andrew felt his hands shaking as he did the same. His eye caught a sudden motion in the street, a cat slinking behind a battered refrigerator box that lay on its side against the building. He could see a person curled up inside, asleep.

Are you sure? Andrew mouthed.

Mom nodded. As she tiptoed to the revolving door, Andrew followed right behind.

She gave it a push, but it was stuck. Andrew eyed a half-open first-floor window and nudged her. She glanced that way and nodded.

They backed away from the revolving door, shoulder to shoulder.

From behind, a hand closed over each of their mouths.

A voice hissed in the darkness, "Don't say a word."

Chapter Fourteen

Evie awoke thinking of Schroeder.

In her dream she was Lucy, lying on a toy piano and listening to Schroeder play. Next to her was a giant bust of Beethoven. But the bust began growing and growing. Its eyes glared at her, its chin poking her in the side. She began losing her balance and tried to push it off. She screamed, pleaded, but it wouldn't yield, until, finally, it shoved *her* off.

She shook off the dream. It was stupid and horrifying at the same time.

But what did it mean? Evie firmly believed that dreams *meant* something.

Schroeder had been playing a song that Mom used to play on the piano. So maybe the dream was really about Mom. But what was with that statue — why was it growing so big? And why Beethoven? Evie didn't know much about him. Just that his music was hard. That he had lost his hearing in adulthood. That he was German, or maybe

Austrian. And that his name was Ludwig. Ludwig Beethoven.

No.

Ludwig *van* Beethoven.

A German, with a van in his name.

Of course! Why hadn't she thought of that before?

Evie grabbed the papers on her night table, nearly knocking off the lamp in her eagerness. She rummaged through them and picked out Andrew's sheet of clues:

When staying strictly in the shade, a scientific premise precedes that which in Yemen is a German van.

A German van. Maybe this clue wasn't talking about *van* as in "moving van." Maybe it mean the *name* type of van.

Mom had taught her that some foreign names had codes — codes that indicated something about the person. Greek names ended in -itis or -opoulos, indicating "child of." Russian middle names ended in -ovitch (son of) or -evyna (daughter of). Other languages had their own codes to indicate if a person was "from" a place, or "of" a person. For the Germans, "van" or "von" did that.

But *Yemen*?

Yemen . . . German?

Think, Evie.

Yemen was an Arabic country. The Arabic culture used codes in their names, too — like the Germans. They had small words than meant "child of" or "descended from." Al. Abu. Ibn.

Abu and *Ibn* each had three letters. Either one would fit. She could pencil one of them in — but where would it go? The clue was the last one on Andrew's sheet. But Mom's last clue was the name of a three-letter school. And then there was Evie's sheet, with a whole other set of clues.

How could there be three sets of clues for one puzzle?

Could it be that all the answers were identical?

It couldn't be. For one thing, Mom's sheet seemed to have many more clues than either of the others.

Were there any similarities at all? Evie glanced from Andrew's clue to her own. Her eyes hovered between each of the very first sentences.

There. His mentioned STRICTLY IN THE SHADE. Hers said AREAS OF LIGHT BETWEEN DARK. The grid had light and dark squares. Could it be that Andrew's answers went in the shaded ones and Evie's in the white ones?

The message on Andrew's sheet was short. Aside from the Yemen/German thing and the part about the shade, there was only one more clue — A SCIENTIFIC PREMISE.

She already had an H and a Y in the first two shaded squares. Hy — what? Hypodermic? Hypochondriac? Those were scientific words.

No. A premise was an idea. A theory. She thought back to her science fair project. She had heated several different types of rock in an oven, then put them in glasses of water and measured the falling temperature, on the hypothesis that the more porous ones would cool faster . . .

Of course!

Evie wrote the word HYPOTHESIS in the shaded boxes, following the dark, spiraling lines.

Only three shaded boxes were left. Those would contain *ibn* or *abu*. How could she know which?

Maybe solving other parts of the puzzle would help her. She noticed that HEY and HYPOTHESIS overlapped. What if she could fill in some more "white box" clues?

She looked at the message Mad Mike had given her:

In areas of light between dark is the bill used between Mediterranean and Baltic, the time occurring between Aug and Oct, and the plunder split between pirates.

Well, *Sep* would be the time between *Aug* and *Oct*. And the last clue could be *spoils* or maybe *bounty*. But . . . the bill used between Mediterranean and Baltic?

"Argggh . . ." Evie groaned. She hated trying to hold it all in her head. It would help to write everything down. She grabbed a pen and scribbled on the bottom of one of the sheets:

Consecutive boxes:
1. A shout that will prick up a horse's ear.   HEY
2. Pull from the ground as you would kill a weed.
3. The cow's in the corn, the _____ in the meadow.   SHEEPS
4. Abbreviated life stories

5. Grain (quick, rolled, or made into meal).
6. A three-letter schl. in a salty four-letter state.

Shaded boxes:

1. A scientific premise   HYPOTHESIS
2. That which in Yemen is a German
    van.   ABU or IBN?

White boxes:

1. Bill used between Mediterranean and Baltic.
2. Time between Aug and Oct.   SEP
3. Plunder split between pirates.   BOUNTY or SPOILS?

There were two places where *sheeps* would fit in consecutive boxes. She could start just to the left of the T. Or
she could start with the S near the center of the puzzle.
But the clue was #3. That meant it must be somewhere in
the midst of the spiraling words, so . . .

"Yes!" Evie exclaimed. The letters for SHEEPS also entered SEP in white boxes. Two clues in one!

Knock-knock-knock.

A sudden pounding at the door made Evie jump. She swept all the sheets off the dresser and put them in a drawer.

"Everyseeng all right in zere?" Ms. Austin's voice called in. "Your fazzer zess you should be zleeping! No zleep, no oatmeal!"

"Okayyyy!" Evie said in a sleepy voice and let out a loud yawn.

But as Ms. Austin's footsteps receded, Evie's mind raced.

Oatmeal.

Made from oats. A grain.

A grain that could be *rolled* and *made into meal*!

Evie pulled out Mom's clue sheet. The exact clue was ONLY THAT ONE WHICH CAN BE QUICK, ROLLED, OR MADE INTO MEAL. So the answer would be *oats* — or maybe the words *only that one* meant that the answer was *oat*. Singular.

She was getting closer. The two most important clues were Clue #2 in the consecutive boxes . . .

PULL FROM THE GROUND AS YOU WOULD KILL A WEED

__P__O__T

And Clue #1 in the white boxes:

BILL USED BETWEEN MEDITERRANEAN AND BALTIC

E _ _ _

Evie shook her head in frustration. A lot of countries sat between the Mediterranean and the Baltic seas. All of Europe did. That was no help.

And what kind of bill? A duck bill . . . a bill of sale . . . a dollar bill?

Wait.

In social studies, they'd talked about currency in Europe. Each country used to have its own separate kind of money, but now there was a common currency.

Euro. That fit perfectly.

Which also filled in the other clue — pull up from the ground: *uproot!*

Nearly there. She was on a roll.

The next clue in consecutive boxes was ABBREVIATED LIFE STORIES:

__I __S

Cinch. Life stories were biographies. Abbreviated — BIOS!

She carefully entered BIOS and the next answer, OAT.

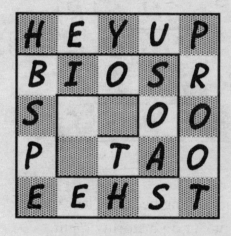

So the pirate plunder (B O O T __) would be *booty*.

And the Yemen equivalent for the German "van" (A __ __) would be *abu*!

Which made the three-letter school in the four-letter state *BYU*. She'd have to look that one up another time.

"Got it!" Evie said

Triumphantly she held out her handiwork:

That which goes out on a stormy night must protect its hands against the cold.

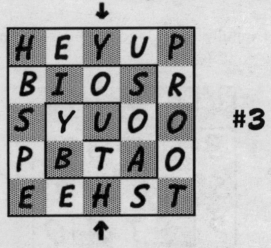

#3

And the whole thing became clear to her:

The fox went out on a stormy night.

You protected your hands with gloves.

Fox. Glove.

Evie's eyes were drawn to the word between the arrows. YOUTH.

And suddenly she knew what she had to do next.

Chapter Fifteen

"Glrp," Andrew said.

The man's hand was tight. He pushed Andrew and Mom into an alleyway beside the building. Andrew struggled to get away, flailing his arms.

"Easy, pal," the man's voice whispered in his ear. "I come in peace."

Mom reached out and held Andrew still. The man's grip loosened. Cautiously they both turned.

Mad Mike's face, mottled with soot, grinned back at them.

"Where'd *you* come from?" Andrew demanded.

Mike put his finger to his mouth. He gestured to the front of the building. The refrigerator box was empty.

"I took over the night shift from a dude named Nails," he whispered. "He didn't know what hit him. Not too smart. Yale guy." He turned and walked toward a pad-locked metal side door. "Okay, follow me, you have work to do."

Andrew looked up at the imposing building. "We're going in there?"

"We have a mole inside — one of our people." He rapped softly on the door, a short but complex rhythm. Then he leaned close to Andrew and slipped him a sheet of paper. "Keep this. You'll need it later, after you find what you need here. Now — listen to my instructions, and move fast."

Up on the third floor, Evie pressed an ear to her door. Silence. Quietly she turned the doorknob. She was afraid that the room would be locked, but it wasn't.

She pulled open the door slowly. The hallway was lit at either end by two bare lightbulbs. She headed to the right.

At the corner she looked for the plastic sign on the wall. It pointed to LODGING, back in the direction from which she'd just come. The other arrow pointed around the corner to her left — YOUTH.

Evie ducked into that hallway. It was shorter. The lightbulb nearest her was dead, and the only illumination was a lonely pool of amber light at the far end. On either side were two rooms behind closed doors, marked 1 to 4.

The spiral crossword had had "#3" written next to it.

Evie approached Room 3 and tapped on the door. No answer. She tapped a little harder.

"Who's there?"

The whispered voice startled her. It came from one of the rooms behind her.

"Foxglove?" Evie whispered back. "I mean, Mrs. Digitalis?"

"*Evie?*"

Room 2.

Evie ran to the door and put her face to it. "It's me. Pop brought me here."

"For goodness sake, dear," Foxglove replied, "do you have the key? The key your mother sent you?"

"No," Evie replied. "Andrew has it. He's at a place called the Ana Mesa. With Mom."

"They kidnapped them, too?"

"They're all right. Pop won't let anything happen to them. It's a misunderstanding. The Company isn't as bad as Mom thinks —"

"Listen to me, Evie," Foxglove interrupted. "Listen closely. Your mother and brother are in great danger. You have been lied to. Dreadfully. They do not intend to treat her lightly — nor me. My door is locked, you see. I'm a prisoner."

"But — but mine was open."

"They want to win your trust. They have plans for you and your code skills. But The Company is in big trouble, my child. They're disbanding San Francisco operations, and they do not want to leave loose ends —"

"No," Evie insisted, her voice rising to a shout. "It's The *Resistance* who are disbanding. The Company discovered Minotaur II!"

"Ssshh, darling, they have sound sensors —"

Bwooop . . . Bwooop . . . Bwooop . . . Bwooop . . .

From every direction came an ear-splitting alarm blast.

"Good heavens, go, Evie!" Foxglove called out over the noise. "Get as far away as you can!"

"What about you?" Evie insisted.

"Just *go!*"

No. She couldn't. Mrs. Digitalis had been there for them when they thought they'd never see Mom again. She'd taught them codes. She'd put her life on the line for them twice — in Connecticut and in San Francisco.

Evie yanked on the doorknob. She heaved her shoulder against the door. But it was solid. Made of metal. The only hope was the hinge. It was an old building. If the hinges were loose, or rusty . . .

She reared back with her right leg and let loose her best Tae Kwon Do kick.

The *thwock* resounded through the hallway. She fell to the floor in excruciating pain. The door hadn't budged.

"*Evie, run!*" Foxglove shouted.

From around the corner came the sound of running footsteps.

It was too late.

Chapter Sixteen

"Get up! Let's go!"

Two silhouettes ran toward her. In the darkness she couldn't make them out, but she knew the voice — Andrew's!

He and Mom emerged into the light. "Come on, Evie!" Andrew shouted.

"But — how did you —?" Evie sputtered.

"Are you all right?" Mom asked, crouching beside her.

"I hurt my leg," Evie said.

"Don't play that game again!" Andrew shouted, pulling her up by the arm. "We have to go!"

"Where is Foxglove?" Mom asked.

"Room 2, Cassandra!" Foxglove's voice piped up.

Mom sprang for the door. In a moment, she'd calibrated the universal key and set Foxglove free.

Evie struggled to her feet as the old woman walked out. "Shall we, dears?" she said, briskly stepping toward the light end of the hallway. She was nearly six feet tall, and her long silvery hair billowed over the broad outlines of her purple outfit. Foxglove always dressed in purple. "The stairs will do," she said over her shoulder, "but we must move at top clip."

She took another turn, pushing open a metal door to a stairwell, and led the way down two flights of stairs. They emerged into a dark room stacked high with boxes. A gang of burly men had formed a chain, passing the boxes to each other en route to a truck waiting in an alleyway.

Foxglove was heading outside. "Wait — we have to get Pop!" Evie insisted.

"Your Pop will not be close by," Foxglove said. "At least not with the workers. And most likely not in the building. He is management, not labor. And labor is always in full force during an evacuation."

"Evacuation?" Andrew asked.

Foxglove threaded her way through the room. The men, intent on their work, didn't seem to notice them at all.

The night air rushed into Evie's lungs as she stepped outside. Foxglove led them quickly through an abandoned lot and onto a side street. Then she turned up a hill — a very steep hill.

The moon had poked its way through the cloud cover, accompanied by a weak canopy of stars. In the distance, Evie could see the searchlight of Coit Tower. Her ankle throbbed. A foghorn moaned in the bay like a wayward cow.

Foxglove stopped at a small park area at the top of the hill. They sat on a bench next to a forlorn-looking swing set. The sand underneath was beginning to glow in the moonlight, or maybe the earliest hints of the not-yet-risen sun.

The old building was not visible from their vantage point, but Evie could hear the truck motors and murmur of voices. "Pop never said anything about an evacuation," she said. "He wouldn't have left me there — and we shouldn't have left him. How do you know there's an evacuation?"

"The Company may have kidnapped me," Foxglove replied, "but I am never without resources. And I had a very valuable one in the building. One who could not have freed me without risk of discovery. I have no doubt your Pop would have returned for you, Evie. But his services were in great demand tonight. You see, his discovery of Minotaur II was not the triumph you assume."

Mom nodded. "The Company had no idea that Minotaur II existed. It scared them."

"Scared them?" Evie said. "But they have their own tunnel complex!"

"*Complex* is a kind word for the antique, low-slung,

poorly ventilated rat trap they use," Foxglove continued. "It's a wonder they don't all have slipped disks and pneumonia. Imagine their faces when your Pop reported that The Resistance had built a well-oiled, state-of-the-art operation —"

"Naturally," Mom said with a smile. "You designed it."

"Well, he received immediate orders to disband!" Foxglove exclaimed. "You see, fear of the unknown is very powerful. Who knew how vast The Resistance tunnels really were? Who knew how long it would take for us to flush them out? The Company believed it was vastly ill-prepared for us."

"Then if The Resistance was so great, why did they close up?" Evie said. "They were uploading info into people's transmitters. Or whatever."

"Precaution," Mom replied. "The Company did discover our location, after all. Any underground headquarters is vulnerable. The release of poison gas, the closing of entrances — it wasn't worth the risk. Besides, if they're moving, then it makes sense for us to move, too."

"But where will The Resistance find someplace as cool as Minotaur II?" Andrew asked.

"O ye of little faith," Foxglove said. "My boy, you don't think I've been sitting on my hands all these years, do you? Remember the documents I shredded back in Connecticut? You were spying on me through your window, as I recall?"

Andrew's blush, at least, was hidden by the darkness.

"Well, some of those papers were hard copies of blueprints," Foxglove went on. "Better tunnel systems than this, in other places."

"Really? Where?" Andrew asked.

"I could tell you," Foxglove replied with a wry glance, "but I'd have to shoot you."

Evie groaned. "So does this mean Pop really did lie? That he doesn't care about us?"

Her answer was a soft foghorn blast and a long, deafening silence.

"He does, Evie," Mom finally replied. "But he's been misguided."

Andrew looked up slowly. His eyes were moist. "Mom? When you leave us again for the new place — who will we stay with?"

Mom seemed surprised at the question. "The Resistance is a movement without a home, Andrew," she said softly. "It's not a place anymore — not yet. Right now, The Resistance is *people*. Literally. Hundreds of them, each carrying a small piece inside, until we can gather again in a physical space. So, you see, the absence of even one person could be catastrophic."

Andrew and Evie nodded. Evie fought back her tears, but Andrew had already lost the battle with his.

"Which is why," Mom continued, "you'll be getting new identities and tutors as we travel."

Her words hung in the air. But they didn't quite hang together. As if Mom had suddenly spoken in Norwegian.

Mom leaned forward. She lifted Andrew's leg onto her lap and rolled up his pants leg so that the moon shone on it. "Have you ever taken a look — a really good look — at your birthmarks?"

Evie angled her own leg. Of course she'd looked at the little blue mark behind her knee. She hated it. It was the reason she didn't like wearing shorts, even though no one ever really noticed the mark but her.

"You mean — I'm —?" Andrew's tears had vanished. A grin spread across his face.

"You mean, this thing is —?" Evie said.

Andrew jumped up. "This is cool! This is soooo cool. I have secret data. I'm . . . a *cyborg*!"

Foxglove let out a hoot of laughter. "Well, no. But you *are* a valuable member of The Resistance."

Evie slumped back on the bench. This wasn't exciting.

This was weird. She and Andrew had embedded transmitters. Some of the uploaded information was in them, too.

They were Resistance now. Like it or not.

She looked at her birthmark curiously. Hadn't it *always* been there? Come to think of it, she couldn't really remember seeing it as a little kid. But she couldn't *not* remember, either. When could they have done this thing?

Evie thought back. "Was it . . . when I had my appendectomy?" she guessed.

Mom nodded. "And when Andrew's tonsils were taken out. While you were unconscious."

"The Resistance has top-notch doctors," Foxglove said.

"I can feel it," Andrew said, tapping his fingers on his knee. "Those gigabytes. They kind of tickle, don't they?"

Evie felt a little sick, thinking of that machine inside her. "What happens after the stuff is downloaded?"

"With or without the data, your lives have changed," Mom replied, "which you've found out. The Company is already after you. They don't give up easily. We'll probably be traveling often. I know you're used to that, but this time we'll have to be careful. New identities. New personal histories to memorize."

A deep, thunderous rumble shook the ground. Mom reached out and held her two kids.

"And an earthquake, too," Andrew exclaimed. "Is this cool or what?"

Foxglove shook her head. "I believe that is the sound of tunnels imploding. And judging from the direction, it's The Company's."

They waited for the motion to subside. From the direction of Oakland, the sun was beginning to color the sky.

"Where do we go now?" Evie asked.

"I'm not sure," Mom said. "But I imagine they'll contact us."

"They already have," Andrew said, digging in his pocket. "Remember? Mad Mike handed us a note before we went into the building. He said we'd need it after we found you guys."

Evie, Mom, and Foxglove gathered around him as he unfolded the note.

Tossed at sea
#1, #2, #3
Limit spins —
Meet begins.

Chapter Seventeen

"Can't make heads or tails of it," Foxglove said. "And I teach the stuff."

"Tossed. Spins," Evie said. "Could it mean tossing and spinning letters — like an anagram? Maybe we rearrange *at sea*?"

Andrew scratched his chin. "I'm not sure. What about the one, two, three?"

"Well, it's not any old one, two, three," Evie said. "It's the three digits, with a number sign near each. Why does that look familiar?"

"I'm trying to figure out *Meet begins*," Andrew said. "It doesn't make any sense . . ."

"Andrew, the *first* code from Mad Mike!" Evie exclaimed. "The Ana Mesa message — do you remember what it said?"

"Of course. *Asian name*."

"But there was more. A number."

Andrew thought back. "You're right. At the bottom

of the screen. A number one. A digit with a little tic-tac-toe sign —"

"Crosshatch."

"Whatever. And there was another one — a number two —"

"On the bites-in-the-donut clue, which told us that Mom was in Room Ten!" Evie said. "And just now, on that weird crossword puzzle that led me to Foxglove, there was a three."

"Does he want us to mix all of those up?" Andrew said. "Why can't he ever he just tell us what he means, straight?"

"Mad Mike lives and breathes codes," Foxglove said. "And for good reason. He knows that anything written can be found."

"What were the answers to the three codes we're talking about?" Mom asked. "Can you write them down — all three answers?"

Evie took out her pen. She turned over Mad Mike's note and wrote on the back:

IN ANA MESA TEN YOUTH

"Makes zero sense," Andrew said.

"Because we have to *toss* it," Evie said. "Unscramble the letters."

"It's a huge string of letters!" Andrew protested. "Where do we begin?"

Mom pointed to the note. "Any hint there?"

Evie stared at it a moment. "*Limit spins . . . meet begins*! He's telling us how to limit the number of rearrangements. And we do that by —"

"Beginning with the word *meet*!" Andrew said. "*Meet begins*!"

Taking a pen from his own pocket, he knelt near Evie. "I'll take the right side, you write on the left. Ready, set, go!"

Mom and Foxglove didn't meddle too much. They patiently looked over the twins' shoulders as they came up with MEET ANTHONY ASUNIA, MEET NATHAN YOUSIAN, MEET ANITA O'SHAUNN . . .

Before long the paper was much brighter than it had been, and Evie realized they'd anagrammed through the sunrise. "I give up," she said.

"There's got to be something, someone . . ." Andrew said, tapping the pencil to his chin. "Did you meet anyone in the building, Evie?"

"Just Pop," Evie replied, "and the Yale guy — Nails. And this weird German lady . . ."

Evie suddenly grabbed the paper. She looked closely at the letters, rearranging them in her head.

Yes.

In big letters, she wrote along the bottom:

MEET YOHANNA AUSTIN

"Well, I'll be," Foxglove said with a funny smile.

"You met her too?" Evie asked.

"Met her?" Foxglove replied. "She's our mole. She's one of us."

They were down the hill in seconds. Evie led the way, with Andrew close behind.

I should have known, Evie said to herself.

"Sheeps . . . I am von Germany" . . . all that talk about oatmeal. Yohanna Austin was giving Evie hints about the crossword.

She was working with Mad Mike.

Evie retraced their path through the alleyway, which looked much less scary in the morning light.

The side door was still open. One last crew of truckers was breaking for coffee and donuts. "You can't go in there!" one of them called out to Evie, reaching out to grab her.

"Hands off, Buster!" Mom said, holding out a flipped-open wallet. There must have been a Company ID inside, because the men instantly retreated.

"They're all gone!" another worker shouted. "You ain't going to find nobody!"

Evie led them into the building's creepy lobby, which was as empty now as it had been earlier.

"Ms. Austin disguises herself as a cleaning lady," Evie said. "She has her own office."

It was easy to remember the location. Just beyond the fluorescent light. Hidden by shadow.

Evie walked carefully inside, felt around for the switch, and flicked on a light.

The place had been cleaned out. Top to bottom. The clothes, the piles of photos, the papers — gone. Empty file cabinet drawers hung open, and a broken fan sat sadly on the windowsill.

In the corner was a tall broom. Evie's eye might have missed it except for the bright yellow Post-It note stuck on the handle.

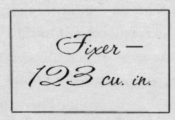

Fixer —
123 cu. in.

She tore it off, her fingers trembling.

Andrew, Mom, and Foxglove came up from behind her. "What is it?" Mom asked.

"Fixer," Foxglove said.

"It's got to be some kind of code," Andrew asked. "The fix is in!"

" 'Fixer' is the title of a book," Foxglove said. "Also a kind of fluid used in photography."

"She was an amateur photographer," Evie said. "What does 'cu. in.' mean?"

"Cubic inches," Andrew piped up.

"Is one hundred twenty-three cubic inches a standard measure?" Mom asked.

"Beats me," Foxglove replied. "I tried photography as a hobby but never could stand the smell."

"This doesn't help us!" Evie said. "We've come this far. We spent all that time decoding Mad Mike's note. We're suppose to meet her. She was going to tell us something. *Where is she*?"

Evie could feel herself starting to unravel. She needed sleep. Lots of sleep.

This note wasn't in code. It was a shopping note. Something she'd written in her capacity as a Company agent. Or as a cleaning lady.

She felt Mom's arm around her shoulder. "Come

on, sweetie. She had to leave. To keep up appearances. She's a double agent. She can never betray their trust."

"If we found her, she might have told us where we were going!" Evie said. "We should have been faster."

"Don't worry, we'll find out soon," Mom said. "They'll contact us."

"Meanwhile, we have a few lovely rented rooms in town where The Company won't find us," Foxglove said. "I suggest some beauty sleep before we tackle our new lives tomorrow."

"New lives," Andrew said dreamily. "Can I be called Anakin? No. Darth. It has a certain ring."

A new identity. Evie wasn't sure how she felt about that. It would mean moving. And secrecy. And tension. It wasn't the way she'd have chosen to end this adventure in her life. There was a lot missing. A lot of sadness.

But they'd be with Mom. Finally. That would feel good.

And who knew? Maybe things with Pop would work out someday.

Anyway, Andrew seemed happy. Ecstatic, even. And sometimes that kind of rubbed off.

"You have the coolest name, Mom," Andrew said. "Spy X. Maybe I could borrow it sometime?"

Evie could feel the rumble of Mom's laugh through her body. "Anytime, Andrew," Mom said. "Anytime."

Time.

They would have a lot of that now.

Evie leaned closer, feeling Mom's warmth.

She could definitely get used to this.

Epilogue

Evie awoke early on November 11.

Except she wasn't Evie any more. She was Jen. Jen Rivers.

It had been nearly two weeks since she, Mom, and Andrew had escaped. Oh. Not Andrew, either. He was Obi. His choice.

Anyway. Grenoble, Wisconsin, hadn't been too bad. Mom had picked it more or less randomly. The kids were nice, and no one asked too many questions about Andrew's weird name or why they'd moved in November or where their dad was. Everyone accepted the notion that Foxglove was an eccentric aunt who'd moved in with the Riverses. They'd even learned to like Wisconsin foods, like cheese and bratwurst.

They hadn't heard a thing from The Resistance. Mom was beginning to worry. But there was always a period of quiet during upheavals, she said, and she hoped they'd be getting their orders soon.

"Pssst, are you awake?" Andrew said, just outside her bedroom door.

"Am now," she replied.

He pushed open the door. "She's in bed."

"Who is?"

"Mom. She's still here. She didn't leave us this time. I've been checking every ten minutes or so."

"All night?"

"I think I dozed off for an hour once."

Evie understood. The memory was fresh for her, too. It had been one year exactly since Mom had left.

Andrew flopped down on her bed. "Do you think it will still be special? Now that's it's not eleven eleven eleven?" he sighed. "I mean, eleven eleven *twelve*? Like, big deal."

"It will be the best birthday ever, and you know it," Evie replied.

Andrew smiled. "You know what I want? Nothing. Just to stay here forever."

"You like Grenoble that much?" Evie couldn't believe the change in her brother. He'd been so . . . *real* lately. Picking "Obi" as a name had been his last Andrew-ish act. Since then, no ridiculous fantasies, no silly names. He had become a normal kind of kid.

She missed the old Andrew.

"Well, I haven't seen a puzzle in weeks, and guess what? I don't miss them. Not at all. I even hate my dumb new name. If I had to do it again, I would have picked Bob. Or Bill. Something normal. I am so into normal right now. I am *Mr.* Normal."

"Well, I'll call you Bob if you really want," Evie said.

The truth was, she missed the puzzles and the excitement. A lot. Every once in a while she found herself looking at the old codes from San Francisco. A couple of them lay on her night table right now. She'd read through them all last night.

"Bob leaves to freshen up for another day at school," Andrew said, hopping off the bed. "See you in the kitchen!"

"I'm going to sleep for seven more minutes," Evie said, flopping down on her pillow.

But her eyes were wide open.

She could hear Mom shuffling downstairs to the kitchen, but that wasn't what was keeping her awake. Andrew's words were bouncing around inside her head.

His normal, Bob words.

See you. Those words.

She reached out to her night table. The spiral puzzle was there, the various messages from Mike. Tricky stuff.

She had finally figured out what BYU stood for — Brigham Young University. It was in Utah — a SALTY FOUR-LETTER STATE because of its famous Salt Lake.

Under Mike's message was Ms. Austin's little Post-It. Evie hadn't bothered to throw that out. Mainly because of that 1, 2, 3. Mad Mike's code had involved a 1, 2, and 3. Coincidence? Maybe. Maybe not. She'd held on just in case.

FIXER. 123 CU. IN.

Cu.

See you.

Cu. In.

See you in.

Evie pulled out their final code, the sheet on which they'd unscrambled MEET YOHANNA AUSTIN. She carefully looked at the letters.

Yes. They were all there.

She crossed the letters of SEE YOU IN out of the message.

MEET YOHANNA AUSTIN

Then she wrote down the remaining letters, in order — MTHANNAAT.

"Oh, wow!" she murmured. "Andrew . . . *Andrew*!"

Her brother bolted into the room. "It's *Bob*."

"Get Mom — *get her right away*!"

"Why? What happened?"

Evie was trembling. "Because we're leaving Wisconsin," she said.

She held out what she'd been working on. And along the bottom, Evie finished the job:

SEE YOU IN MANHATTAN

"M-Manhatt — as in New York City?" Andrew exclaimed.

"Are you still Bob?" Evie said.

"Are you *nuts*?"

They were out the room in a shot. Racing to the kitchen. To the birthday they'd been waiting for.

To eleven eleven twelve.

To their future.